Dear Reader,

Welcome to the town of Hard Luck, Alaska! I hope you'll join me there to meet the Midnight Sons, their families, friends and wives-to-be.

The people I want to credit with the idea for this project are, in fact, fictional—they're Valerie, Stephanie and Norah, the three sisters I wrote about in the *Orchard Valley* trilogy (Harlequin Romance #3232, #3239, #3244). I loved writing those books, I loved the characters and the town and last but definitely not least, I loved the way readers responded to the stories.

So when Harlequin suggested this six-book project, I was thrilled. Soon after that, the town of Hard Luck, the O'Halloran brothers and Midnight Sons all came to life. Never have I worked harder on a project, nor have I enjoyed my research more. In the summer of 1994, my husband and I traveled to Alaska, and I fell in love with the state—its sheer magnificence, the warmth of its people, the excitement of life on the "last frontier."

Now I invite you to sit back, put your feet up and allow me to introduce you to some proud, stubborn, *wonderful* men—Alaskan men—and show you what happens when they meet their real matches—women from the lower forty-eight. Women with the courage to change their lives and take risks for love. Women a lot like you and me!

Love,

Debbie

P.S. The books are

Brides for Brothers
The Marriage Risk
Daddy's Little Helpe
Because of the Baby
Falling for Him
Ending in Marriage

D1024158

Debbie Macomber is one of the most popular romance authors writing today. She's written more than seventy romances (for Harlequin and Silhouette) and several bestselling "mainstream" women's fiction novels. Not surprisingly, Debbie has won a number of awards for her books.

She lives in Washington State with her husband, Wayne, and their dog, Peterkins. They have four grown children—and they've just become grandparents! Debbie's *thrilled* with her new granddaughter, Jazmine Lynn.

Debbie loves to hear from her readers. You can reach her at: P.O. Box 1458, Port Orchard, Washington 98366.

Books by Debbie Macomber

HARLEQUIN ROMANCE

Midnight Sons is a six-book series. The titles are:

Don't miss any of our special offers. Write to us at the following address for information on our newest releases.

Harlequin Reader Service
U.S.: 3010 Walden Ave., P.O. Box 1325, Buffalo, NY 14269
Canadian: P.O. Box 609, Fort Erie, Ont. L2A 5X3

MIDNIGHT SONS

DEBBIE MACOMBER

Because of the Baby

Harlequin Books

TORONTO • NEW YORK • LONDON
AMSTERDAM • PARIS • SYDNEY • HAMBURG
STOCKHOLM • ATHENS • TOKYO • MILAN
MADRID • WARSAW • BUDAPEST • AUCKLAND

ISBN 0-373-03395-8

BECAUSE OF THE BABY

First North American Publication 1996.

This edition published by arrangement with Harlequin Books S.A.

Printed in U.S.A.

The History of Hard Luck, Alaska

Hard Luck, situated fifty miles north of the Arctic Circle, near the Brooks Range, was founded by Adam O'Halloran and his wife, Anna, in 1931. Adam came to Alaska to make his fortune, but never found the gold strike he sought. Nevertheless, the O'Hallorans and their two young sons, Charles and David, stayed on—in part because of a tragedy that befell the family a few years later.

Other prospectors and adventurers began to move to Hard Luck, some of them bringing wives and children. The town became a stopping-off place for mail, equipment and supplies. The Fletcher family arrived in 1938 to open a dry goods store.

When World War II began, Hard Luck's population was fifty or sixty people, all told. Some of the young men, including the O'Halloran sons, joined the armed services; Charles left for Europe in 1942, David in 1944 at the age of eighteen. Charles died during the fighting. Only David came home—with a young English war bride, Ellen Sawyer (despite the fact that he'd become engaged to Catherine Fletcher shortly before going overseas).

After the war, David qualified as a bush pilot. He then built some small cabins to attract the sport fishermen and hunters who were starting to come to Alaska; he also worked as a guide. Eventually, in the early seventies, he built a lodge to replace the cabins— a lodge that later burned.

David and Ellen had three sons, born fairly late in their marriage—Charles (named after David's brother) was born in 1960, Sawyer in 1963 and Christian in 1965.

Hard Luck had been growing slowly all this time, and by 1970 it was home to just over a hundred people. These were the years of the oil boom, when the school and community center were built by the state. After Vietnam, ex-serviceman Ben Hamilton joined the community and opened the Hard Luck Café, which became the social focus for the town.

In the late 1980s, the three O'Halloran brothers formed a partnership, creating Midnight Sons, a bush-pilot service. They were awarded the mail contract, and also delivered fuel and other necessities to the interior. In addition, they serve as a small commuter airline, flying passengers to and from Fairbanks and within the North Arctic.

At the time these stories start, there are approximately 150 people living in Hard Luck—a preponderance of them male....

PROLOGUE

SHE WOULD ALWAYS BE his valentine, according to the card.

The man was a low-down, dirty rat! Furiously Karen Caldwell tossed the card into the garbage. She stood there in the middle of her kitchen, with the Californian sun pouring through her windows, and battled down tears.

Leave it to her ex-husband to do something like this. In the four years of their marriage Matt hadn't once bought her a valentine card. *Or* an anniversary card. Oh, no, he waited until they were divorced to do that. Waited until she was convinced he was finally out of her life—and her heart. Only then had he bothered to send her a card. A sweet, funny card celebrating a day meant for lovers. He'd purposely postponed contacting her until she'd managed to persuade herself she was almost happy.

Karen drew a deep, shaky breath, determined to put the man and the valentine out of her mind.

Her ex-husband infuriated her. This was just another example. Put a hundred, a thousand, of these examples together, and it explained why she'd divorced him. Matthew Caldwell was irresponsible. Thoughtless. Unreliable. In the four years of their marriage he'd changed careers five times. Five times!

Without fail, whenever she'd begun to think he'd finally found his niche, Matt would casually announce he'd quit his job. Not once had he discussed his plans with her.

He seemed to believe his decision was none of her concern.

Over and over he'd tell her he didn't know how unhappy he was until the moment he quit, as if that should be all the explanation she'd need.

Giving his notice at Curtis Accounting had been the final straw. When that happened Karen had done the only sensible thing a woman could do in the circumstances. She left him.

No one blamed her, least of all Matt's family. His parents and sister were as exasperated with his penchant for shifting careers as she was herself.

Right after the divorce Karen had been offered the transfer to California. Leaving Alaska just then had sounded like a perfect solution, and it didn't hurt that a promotion went along with the relocation. The move was sure to help her put the unpleasantness of her failed marriage behind her. Sunny California was just the distraction she needed.

Or so Karen had thought.

Now she wasn't so sure. She missed Alaska. Missed her friends. And damn it all, she missed Matt.

Karen avoided looking at the garbage can. Every time she thought of the valentine card, it made her mad. What irritated her most was that she knew he'd had to go out of his way to buy it.

Karen had been to Hard Luck, where Matt was living now. In a town that small, there wouldn't be anyplace that sold greeting cards. Matt would've had to order it by mail, or fly into Fairbanks.

He'd moved to Hard Luck because of the lodge—his latest folly.

Karen rolled her eyes at the thought. Her ex-husband had used the trust fund his grandmother had left him to purchase the burned-out lodge from the O'Halloran brothers. What Karen understood from a conversation with his sister was that Matt had begun to renovate it and hoped to attract tourists. Tourists north of the Arctic Circle!

But then, it made as much sense as anything else Matt had done in the past few years. If he wanted to waste his inheritance on another one of his grand schemes, *she* wouldn't try to stop him. Besides, it was none of her business.

When she couldn't stand it any longer Karen pulled the valentine out of the garbage. Below the printed message, he'd written "love" and his name.

Tears blurred her eyes. If this was how she reacted to a simple card, what would happen at the wedding? Matt's sister, Lanni, had asked Karen to serve as her maid of honor, and she'd agreed.

True, it might be a bit uncomfortable, since Matt was attending the wedding, but Lanni had assured her that she'd discussed the situation with him. Matt hadn't objected. They might be divorced, but they were both adults.

It had been eighteen months since she'd last seen her exhusband. The wedding wouldn't be so bad, Karen decided. She'd smile a lot and let him know how happy she was. How much she liked California. How well she was doing at her job.

She'd make sure she looked her best, too. Lose five pounds, get her hair trimmed, buy some new clothes. After one glance, he'd be ready to hand her his heart on a silver platter.

And Karen? She'd hand it right back.

CHAPTER ONE

"SHE'S JUST BEAUTIFUL," Pearl Inman whispered to Matt as his sister walked down the center aisle, escorted by their proud father. "A perfect spring bride."

"Yes, she is," Matt agreed, but his eyes weren't on Lanni. He hadn't been able to stop watching Karen from the moment she'd entered the church.

Matt had been too busy getting the lodge ready for his first guests to give much thought to his sister's wedding. He knew Lanni had asked his ex-wife to serve as her maid of honor. He'd gone so far as to assure her it didn't matter to him. He'd managed to sound downright nonchalant about it, too.

It wasn't any big deal, he'd told Lanni. Their marriage was over. Finished. Kaput. Nope, it wouldn't bother him if Karen came to Hard Luck. He didn't plan to give it another thought.

All right, if he was being honest—and he should be, since he was in a church—he *had* thought about Karen coming to Hard Luck. Okay, so he'd counted the days. The hours. The minutes. But he wasn't going to beat himself up because of it. They'd been married for four years and divorced nearly two. It was only natural he'd be anxious about seeing her.

To his dismay, Matt soon discovered he was completely unprepared for the emotional impact of being with Karen again.

Especially at a wedding.

Damn, she was beautiful. His heart ached just looking at her. She wore an elegant rose-colored dress that was perfect for her tall, lithe frame. A halo of flowers circled her glossy brown hair and Matt was convinced he'd never seen a more beautiful maid of honor.

A more beautiful woman.

The church was packed. It surprised and pleased Matt that Lanni and Charles had decided to be married in Hard Luck. He'd assumed his sister would choose Anchorage, where the majority of their friends and family lived. When he'd asked her, Lanni said she'd chosen Hard Luck since this was where she and Charles would make their home. She'd met and fallen in love with Charles O'Halloran here, so it seemed fitting to have the wedding here, as well. In time, Lanni hoped to start a community newspaper, but until Hard Luck was large enough to support a weekly, she'd be content to write free-lance articles.

Matt was happy for his sister. He didn't doubt that Charles and Lanni were deeply in love. But watching them together had been almost painful. Their closeness, their delight in each other—he remembered what those feelings were like. Before his marriage fell apart...

With effort Matt pulled his gaze away from Karen.

This winter had been a long bleak one, with only his hopes for the lodge to sustain him.

The wedding was the one bright spot in an otherwise bleak winter. It would be another six weeks before the snow melted. Another month before he got any response to the advertising he'd mailed to travel agencies around the country.

Matt had risked a whole lot more than his inheritance in buying the lodge. He closed his eyes, refusing to allow any worries to crowd his mind. On the positive side, every room had been booked for the night. Never mind that his guests were family and friends and that he wasn't getting a dime for his hospitality. Never mind that his ex-wife was one of those guests.

The wedding was a sort of dry run for the lodge. Unfortunately the kitchen wasn't in working order yet, but he'd have everything up and running by mid-June. Just in time to welcome his first real customers.

Love. Honor. As Charles O'Halloran repeated his vows, Matt felt a wrenching ache in his chest. He'd purposely let his mind wander in an effort to avoid just this.

The marriage vows were a painful reminder of how he'd failed Karen. Difficult as it was to admit, he'd never been the right husband for her. She wanted a man who was content to hold down a nine-to-five job. A husband who'd work forty years for the same company and retire with a decent pension.

Matt had tried to give her the stability she'd craved. It just hadn't worked. Within months of taking on a job, he'd grow restless and bored. He'd always brought real effort and creativity to every new position; if he put that kind of effort into something, Matt wanted to be the one who profited from the outcome. Karen had never understood or appreciated that.

Lanni's sweet voice echoed Reverend Wilson's words. His sister's eyes lovingly held her husband's. It was a poignant moment, and more than one person was fighting back tears. Charles and Lanni had bridged the pain and anger of two families to find happiness. The O'Hallorans and Catherine Fletcher—Matt and Lanni's grandmother—had become bitter and enduring enemies when Charles's father married another woman. But the enmity was over now. And it was largely due to Lanni, Matt reflected, looking at her with pride.

Despite his best effort, his eyes wandered back to Karen. Her head was bowed as if she, too, had a hard time listening to the exchange of vows.

They hadn't spoken since her arrival in Hard Luck. He didn't think she was actually avoiding him, but he couldn't be sure. Her flight had landed in Fairbanks early that morning; Sawyer O'Halloran had picked her up, along with the other two bridesmaids, who'd flown in from Anchorage. The three women had been closeted with Lanni ever since, getting ready for the wedding.

He knew Karen was scheduled to fly out first thing the next morning. But for this one night she'd be sleeping in the lodge. *His* lodge.

Matt had made sure when he assigned the rooms that Karen got the most elaborate one. The one with the big brass bed and feather mattress. He'd polished the hardwood floor himself until it shone like new. Matt wondered if she'd guess all the trouble he'd gone to—then decided he didn't want her to know.

The ceremony was soon over, and Matt heaved a sigh of relief. Nothing like a wedding to remind him of his own shortcomings in the husband department. In failing Karen, he'd failed himself.

He and Karen had once been as much in love as Lanni and Charles. In fact, he'd still loved her when she left him and filed for divorce. And despite everything, he loved her now.

His jaw tightened as he remembered the night he'd come home to find she'd packed her bags and moved out—and then had him served with the divorce papers. It rankled to this day that she hadn't so much as talked to him first.

He'd asked her about that once, and she'd shrugged as if it was of little concern. She'd warned him, she'd said.

Besides, he'd never talked to *her* about quitting his jobs. Now it was his turn to see how it felt.

In all these months his bitterness hadn't faded. It would be best if they didn't talk to each other, Matt decided. Nothing would be served by dredging up the past, especially when that was all they had to discuss.

Music crescendoed, filling the church as Lanni and Charles turned to greet their guests. His sister's face radiated happiness. Arm in arm, the couple strolled down the aisle.

Karen followed with Sawyer O'Halloran, one of Charles's younger brothers. It didn't escape Matt's notice that his ex-wife did everything humanly possible to avoid looking in his direction.

So she didn't want any eye contact? Well, he wasn't too keen on it himself. This whole affair was difficult enough without their having to confront each other. He'd managed to get through the wedding; now all he needed to do was survive the reception. That shouldn't be so difficult.

It took Matt all of ten minutes to retract those words.

He delayed going to the school gymnasium, where the reception was being held, as long as he could. By the time he arrived, the music had started and a half-dozen couples were already on the area cleared for dancing.

The first person Matt saw was Karen—dancing with Duke Porter, one of the pilots for Midnight Sons, the Arctic flight service owned and run by the O'Hallorans. The sight of another man with his arms around Karen made Matt so damn mad he walked directly over to the bar and downed a glass of champagne. He wasn't sure that getting drunk would serve a useful purpose, but it might help cut the pain. This probably wasn't the first time a man had held her since their divorce, but it was the only time he'd been around to witness it. He didn't like the experience one bit.

"Where were you?" The question came from his mother, Kate. "I was beginning to get worried."

"I'm fine." It was another moment or two before he could pull his gaze away from Karen and Duke. "I, uh, was making sure everything was ready at the lodge."

"Your aunt Louise is looking for you."

Matt didn't bother to disguise a groan. "Mother, please, anyone but Aunt Louise." The first thing his meddling aunt would do was quiz him about his divorce. Matt figured he'd need more than one glass of champagne if he was going to be trapped in a conversation with his father's oldest sister. He doubted an entire bottle would fortify him for Aunt Louise and her shamelessly prying questions.

His rescue came from the most unlikely source. Chrissie Harris, eight-year-old daughter of Mitch, the town's public-safety officer.

"Will you dance with me?" the child pleaded, widening her dark, seal-pup eyes.

"Sure thing, kiddo." He grinned. The kid's timing couldn't have been better.

"Dad's dancing with Bethany," Chrissie explained, sounding a little disappointed. "Dad and Bethany are getting married this summer."

Great, another wedding. "I know."

"I think Scott would like to ask me, but he's afraid." Scott was Sawyer O'Halloran's adopted ten-year-old son— one of his wife's two children by a previous marriage.

Matt held out his arms to the girl. "Well, we can't let the prettiest girl here be a wallflower," he said. Mitch's daughter slipped off her patent-leather Mary Janes and stepped onto the tops of his shoes. He waltzed her from one end of the dance floor to the other. For a whole minute, perhaps longer, he was able to enjoy the dance without thinking of Karen.

His pleasure was short-lived, however. The next time he happened to catch sight of her, Karen was with Christian O'Halloran, Charles and Sawyer's younger brother. At the end of the dance, Matt thanked Chrissie and refilled his glass.

The second glass of champagne gave him enough courage to approach his ex-wife. It was ridiculous to pretend they weren't aware of each other.

Karen was sitting, probably for the first time since the music had started. He picked up two full champagne glasses and walked over to her. Although she wasn't looking in his direction, she knew he was coming. Matt could tell by the way her body stiffened.

"Hello, Karen," he said evenly.

"Matt."

He handed her one of the glasses and claimed the empty seat beside her. "You look like you could use something to drink."

"Thanks."

Neither seemed to have anything more to say. Matt struggled to find some safe, neutral topic.

"How's California?" he managed finally.

She stared into the champagne as if she expected to find her response written in the bottom of the glass. "Wonderful."

"You look good." It was best to start off with a compliment, he decided; besides, it was the truth. She looked fantastic.

"You, too."

It was nice of her to lie. He'd lost fifteen pounds because he'd been working his butt off for months. He rarely got enough sleep and wasn't eating properly.

She took a sip of champagne, then asked, "Why'd you mail me a valentine card?" He thought her voice shook ever so slightly.

He regretted sending that stupid thing the moment he'd slipped it into the mailbox. If there'd been a way to retrieve it, he would have.

"We were married for four years," she said, "and not once in all that time did you buy me a card."

He didn't have an argument, so he said nothing.

"You claimed cards were silly commercial sentiments, remember?"

He wasn't likely to forget.

"Why this year?" she demanded, and the tremble in her voice was more apparent than ever.

"Maybe I was trying to make up for the years I didn't give you one." It wasn't much of an explanation, but the only one he had to offer. When he hadn't heard back from her—not that he'd expected to—Matt knew she hadn't appreciated the gesture.

"Don't mail me any more...sentiments, Matt. It's too little and it's much too late."

He frowned. "Fine, I won't."

They both stood up, eager to escape one another. Unfortunately they came face-to-face with his aunt Louise. Karen looked to Matt to rescue her, but he was fresh out of ideas.

"Dance, you two."

Aunt Louise issued the order like a drill sergeant. The woman always did enjoy meddling in other people's affairs. It was either follow her dictates or be trapped in a thirty-minute question-and-answer ordeal.

Karen glanced at Matt and he stared at her. "Shall we?" he asked, motioning toward the dance floor. Judging by the look she gave him, Karen had weighed her choices and decided that dancing with him was the lesser of two evils.

Matt had often observed that when one thing went wrong, others were sure to follow. The music, which to this point had been fast and lively, abruptly changed to something slow and soft. Matt couldn't avoid touching Karen, nor could he avoid holding her close.

He slipped his arm around her waist and she held herself stiffly in his embrace. Matt did his utmost to concentrate on moving to the slow beat of the music and not on the woman in his arms.

He could feel her reluctance with every step.

"Don't worry," he whispered, "I promise not to bite."

"Your bites don't worry me."

"What does?" he asked.

"Everything else."

He smiled to himself and unconsciously moved his head closer to hers until his jaw pressed against her temple. Matt never had been light on his feet, but when he danced with Karen he somehow managed to look as though he knew what he was doing. It was as though the two of them were born partners.

Neither spoke for the rest of the dance. The second the music stopped he released her and stepped back. The ache in his chest intensified, and he wondered how much longer he'd have to stay at the reception. He didn't want to slight his sister and brother-in-law, but being with Karen was pure agony. Pretending he didn't still love her was becoming impossible.

"Lanni and Charles are getting ready to leave," Karen said quickly. He sensed that she felt as awkward as he did. "I'd better see if she needs my help."

"Thanks for the dance."

Her eyes briefly met his and filled with an unmistakable sadness. "It was good to see you again, Matt," she mumbled, then hurried away.

Much as he longed to escape, Matt observed the proprieties—he kissed his sister and shook hands with Charles. They were honeymooning in the Virgin Islands for two weeks. He wished them a great trip, made the rounds to say his farewells and returned to the lodge.

Because he felt about as low as he ever had since his divorce, he brought out a dusty bottle of whiskey and poured himself a stiff drink. He wasn't a drinking man, but there were times when little else would do.

This was one of those times.

He sat on the leather sofa in front of the massive stone fireplace, his feet propped up on the raised hearth. He held the glass in one hand and the bottle in the other.

Soon his guests began to arrive. His parents came in first. It had been a long, exhausting day, and after a few words of greeting, they wandered up the stairs. The two bridesmaids followed and then another couple, married friends of Lanni's.

Karen was the last to arrive. Matt didn't ask who'd escorted her to the lodge. Probably Duke, but he didn't want to hear that.

She paused in the large hall and looked around. Plenty of work remained to be done, but it was a pleasant, inviting room. Besides the sofa, Matt had placed a couple of big overstuffed chairs close to the fireplace. The other half of the room was set up with hardwood tables and chairs.

"This is very nice," Karen said, sounding surprised.

"Thanks." He'd worked damn hard, getting this place in presentable shape. For just a moment he wondered what she thought when she heard he'd purchased the lodge.

Years before, a fire had destroyed much of the kitchen, plus a number of rooms upstairs.

Following the fire, the O'Hallorans had boarded up the place, unable to decide what to do with it. So the lodge had sat vacant and deteriorating for years. None of the brothers was interested in running a tourist business, and repairs would've been costly and time-consuming.

"Your room's at the top of the stairs. The farthest one down on the left-hand side." He gestured with the shot glass, afraid that if he stood, he might fall over.

"You've been drinking." Karen moved closer to the fireplace.

"Nothing gets past you, does it?" he muttered, too drunk to bother keeping the sarcasm out of his voice.

"You hardly ever drink." The problem was, the woman knew him too well.

"That's true, but sometimes the occasion calls for it." He raised his glass to her with a sardonic smile and downed the last of the whiskey. It burned a trail down the back of his throat. He squeezed his eyes shut, clenched his teeth and shook his head like a wet dog.

When he opened his eyes Karen sat on the other end of the sofa. "What's wrong?" she asked gently—as if she didn't know.

"Nothing," he answered cheerfully. "What could possibly be wrong?"

She didn't make the obvious reply. "I think I must have had a little more to drink than usual myself." Her eyes seemed unnaturally bright.

She got up and headed toward the stairs, and Matt realized he didn't want her to leave. "Do you want to see what I've spent the last few months doing?" he asked.

"Sure." Her eager response surprised him.

He gave her a quick tour of the downstairs area, pointing out the renovations. He was pleased with them, and didn't conceal his pride. "The kitchen should be ready soon," he explained when he'd finished showing her around. "The stove's what's holding me up, but I expect it in the next month or so."

"Who's going to do the cooking?" she asked.

"Right now, me." Matt shrugged. "I don't have a budget to hire anyone else. At least not yet. It's important to bring in paying guests first."

"Well, you're certainly qualified to cook."

She was referring to his stint as a chef. He'd enjoyed cooking school well enough, but had lost interest during his first restaurant job. He'd gone on to commercial fishing shortly after that, abandoning his sketchy plans to open a restaurant of his own.

"I wish you the very best with this venture, Matt."

"Thanks." He knew he sounded flippant.

"I mean that," she insisted.

He'd probably offended her, and he hadn't meant to. "But you don't believe it'll last, do you?"

"No." She didn't so much as hesitate. "You'll grow bored with the lodge just like you did with everything else."

"Maybe." He wasn't going to argue with her. Time would prove her wrong. He'd worked harder on this lodge than anything he'd done in his life. For the first time, he had something that was entirely his. The business would sink or succeed by his own efforts, no one else's.

"I'll show you to your room," he said without emotion, and led the way to the staircase.

He hadn't gone more than a few steps when she stopped him. "Matt." His arm tingled where her fingers touched him. "I apologize—I didn't mean to discourage you. I can tell you've put a lot of thought and effort into this lodge. I hope it succeeds. I really do."

He turned to face her. "Do you, Karen?"

Her eyes had never been more intent. In them he found a reflection of the loneliness he'd felt these past eighteen months. He hadn't wanted to admit, even to himself, how much he'd missed her. For months he'd worked himself into a state of exhaustion, rather than face a night without her.

This evening, for the first time since their divorce, he was forced to admit how good it felt to hold her. He couldn't deny how empty his arms felt without her. How empty his *life* felt.

Her face was slightly flushed. She still wore the rose-colored dress. The neckline was scooped, and it was impossible to ignore the gentle thrust of her breasts.

"I've missed you, Karen." She must know what it had cost him to admit that.

Her eyes drifted shut, and when she spoke her voice was so low the words were hardly discernible. "I've missed you, too."

His breath caught in his throat, and Matt figured if he didn't touch her soon he'd die. He raised his hand and cradled her cheek with his callused palm. She was so smooth, so soft.

Karen moistened her lips.

It was the invitation Matt had been waiting for. He drew her toward him, and to his surprise, to his delight, she came without resistance.

He was almost afraid to kiss her, fearing she'd pull away from him, fearing she'd throw the past in his face. Karen did neither. When she brought her arms up to circle his neck, Matt nearly shouted for joy.

He didn't give her time to object. His kiss was raw with need. He'd intended to be gentle, to coax her, but it wasn't what either of them wanted. He possessed her mouth. No other words described their kiss. His lips slanted over hers, twisting, seeking, urgently needing the taste of her.

When her lips parted in unspoken welcome, he groaned and thrust his tongue deep into the waiting warmth.

Controlling the kiss was beyond him. Matt didn't know how long it continued. Too long. *Much* too long, he decided. When he did find the strength to ease his mouth from hers, they were both breathless.

He held her and waited for her to say something. Like telling him he shouldn't have done that. Perhaps she expected an apology. If so, she wouldn't be getting one.

He felt her shift, and afraid that she was about to move out of his arms, he tightened his grip. She snuggled close to him, creating a new kind of torture. They'd been intimate too many years for him not to be affected by the sensation of her body stirring against his.

When she ran her tongue along the underside of his jaw Matt was forced to pull away. They stared at each other. Neither spoke, and he suspected it was because they both feared what the other would say. Her lips were moist and slightly swollen; her breath came in soft, disjointed gasps, as if she was struggling not to weep. His own was ragged and made a light hissing sound through his clenched teeth.

He kissed her again and this time forced himself to keep it slow and gentle. But when he ended the kiss the sensual impact had stripped him of all his painfully gathered control. He pulled her close against him, knowing she'd feel his arousal.

"I never was much good at these kinds of games," he said, his eyes holding hers.

"Games?"

"You know what I mean."

She lowered her lashes and her face filled with color.

"Don't expect me to silently steer you into my bedroom," he said. "If we're going to make love, I need to know you want me as much as I want you."

Still she said nothing.

"What's it to be, Karen? You can share my bed or go upstairs alone." The temptation to kiss her again was strong, but he resisted.

Tears brightened her eyes, and she bit her lower lip. "I don't want to be alone," she whispered.

He shook his head. "That's not good enough. Tell me you want me."

"Yes," she said stiffly, "I want you, Matt. I've missed you."

CHAPTER TWO

KAREN AWOKE with Matt's arm securely tucked around her waist. In the carefree state between sleep and complete wakefulness, she reveled in the comfort of being held in her husband's arms.

Husband.

It took her far longer than it should have to remember that he *wasn't* her husband. Not anymore. Her eyes flew open as her brain started putting together the events of the night before.

The wedding.

She was in Hard Luck for Lanni and Charles's wedding. She should never have agreed to serve as Lanni's maid of honor. That had been her first mistake. The divorce had been final for more than eighteen months. Karen had thought, no, hoped that any lingering emotion she carried for Matt was long dead. Her reaction to the valentine card should have told her otherwise. If she'd had a whit of common sense, she'd have phoned Lanni and begged off. Instead, she'd set out to prove she was over Matt.

She'd proved that all right, by spending the night with him. Mortified, Karen closed her eyes and forced back a sob. She'd had more to drink than usual, but she hadn't been even close to drunk, and she knew it.

She wanted to blame Matt for this. In fact, she'd feel a whole lot better if she could accuse him of seducing her, of

luring her into his bedroom. But bless his black heart, he'd
made sure she knew exactly what she was doing before
they'd gone to bed.

The lovemaking had been incredible. It had always been
good between them, but she'd forgotten just how good.
They'd been so hungry for each other, so needy.

Afterward, Matt had held her in his arms and she'd silently wept. Not because she felt any regrets—she hadn't,
not then. But because she had to admit how miserable
she'd been without him. It wasn't fair; she loved him so
much, yet she realized how wrong they were for each other.
Just as her own mother must have realized at some point
how wrong her own marriage had gone, how mismatched
she and Karen's father were. Yet she'd steadfastly hung on
for reasons Karen had never understood.

She and Matt had such contradictory expectations and
needs. She had to have some predictability in her life, some
certainty. He preferred just to drift along, following his
whims. Of course, she hadn't known, when she first met
him, that he'd have trouble staying in a job. It wasn't until after they were married that he started his pattern of
changing from one occupation to the next. Karen felt
blindsided.

Every time Matt quit a job, Karen faced an unhappy
memory from her childhood. Her father had shared the
same lack of ambition. Her mother's meager paycheck had
supported the family. It wasn't that Eric Rocklin was lazy;
far from it. His garden had been the neighborhood show-
piece, and his model airplanes won contests. He was a
good father, an attentive husband, a decent person.

His one failing was his inability to keep at a job.

Her family had declared bankruptcy when Karen and
her brother were in high school. One of her most humili-
ating memories was of the time her friends were visiting

and two men came to repossess the family car. Later they were turned out of their rental house.

From the moment she introduced them, Matt and her father had gotten along famously. Now Karen knew why. As the saying goes, they were two peas in a pod.

Wearily she closed her eyes. She refused to make the same mistakes her mother had, refused to allow her husband's weakness to destroy her future. Painful though it was, she'd taken the necessary steps to correct the problem and get on with her life.

One small lapse wasn't the end of the world. It was only natural, she decided, to still have feelings for Matt. He was a gracious, compassionate person. And she was undeniably attracted to him. But he wasn't right for her. She'd put their night together behind her and go back to California, her lesson well learned. The farther away she was from Matt the better.

As carefully as she could, Karen folded back the covers and slipped one leg over the edge of the mattress. She eased herself from under Matt's arm and glanced around for something to cover herself. She caught sight of her dress, carelessly discarded in last night's haste; it lay crumpled on the floor across the room. She blushed, remembering how eager they'd been for each other. They hadn't been able to remove their clothes fast enough.

"Mornin'," Matt rolled onto his back, stretched his arms high above his head and yawned.

Karen rolled back into bed, covered herself with the sheet and ground her teeth in frustration. She'd hoped to be gone by the time Matt awoke.

Her ex-husband slid over to her side and propped up his head with one hand. "Did I ever tell you how beautiful you look in the morning?"

"No." She wanted to groan aloud. It would have saved them both a good deal of embarrassment if she could've silently slunk away.

"Then let me correct that error." Brushing the hair from her face, he bent forward to kiss her gently. "You're beautiful in the morning. You brighten my life, Karen. Without you—"

"Don't say it. Please don't say it."

"Don't say it?"

"Last night was a mistake," she said coldly.

Matt looked stunned. "That's not what you said when—"

"I was drunk," she interrupted him, offering the first excuse that came to mind, although she'd already rejected it earlier.

He laughed harshly. "And pigs fly. Neither one of us had *that* much to drink."

"But enough—"

"Yes," he said, "enough to loosen our inhibitions. It was a good thing, too, because we belong together, Karen. We always have. I never did understand why you left me."

His words reminded her of the decision she'd already made—the decision to leave again. And why. "That says it all, don't you think?"

He ignored her question, something he'd often done. "Sure you were upset about me quitting my job, but I hated it. Would you really want me to continue working someplace that made me miserable?"

"Yes!" she cried. It was too late for this, but he'd drawn her in the way he always had. "If it was the first time I wouldn't have cared, although you might have talked it over with me, but it *wasn't* the first time. It was the fourth time in as many years, and now you're running a lodge. You'll never find the perfect job. Twenty years from now you'll still be searching for a career that suits you. Nothing's going to change.''

"Come off it, Karen. I'm only thirty-one."

"I don't have the time or energy to argue with you." There was no other option, so she tossed back the sheets and hurried across the room to retrieve her dress. With the zipper in the back, she had two choices—to either ask him to close it for her, or scurry to her room with the dress gaping open. She chose the latter.

"All right, all right," he muttered, lying on his back and staring at the ceiling. "I don't want to argue with you, either."

As fast as she could Karen gathered together the rest of her things, stuffing them in her arms.

"You aren't leaving, are you?" He sounded shocked.

"Yes." The sooner she retreated to her room, the better. Then she'd change clothes and get out of here.

"What about last night?"

Karen didn't know what to tell him. "Let's say it was for old times' sake."

His jaw tightened. "Do you do this sort of thing often?"

It would have hurt less if he'd punched her in the stomach. "That was a cheap shot, Matt, and unworthy of you. You've been my only lover and you damn well know it." Then, with as much dignity as she could marshal, she marched barefoot out of his bedroom. Halfway up the stairs she met Matt's parents. They stared at her, mouths open.

"Good morning," she greeted as if she were dressed for a church meeting, ignoring the panty hose and underthings bunched in her arms.

"Karen." Matt's father nodded; his mother managed a belated good-morning.

As she continued up the stairs, Karen heard Kate call out to her son. "Matt, is everything all right with you and Karen?"

Matt didn't respond right away. "Nothing's changed."

His father's warm chuckle followed Karen into her room. "You could've fooled me."

TWO HOURS LATER, Karen was sitting in the Midnight Sons mobile office, waiting for the pilot to fly her out of Hard Luck. She stared at the worn floor, impatient to be gone and fully aware of why.

Matt made her weak when she believed she was strong.

Pressing her hands to her face, Karen closed her eyes and drew several deep, calming breaths. It was better for them both that she lived in California now. The temptation to be with him would be too great if she'd stayed in Alaska. Even Anchorage, which was hundreds of miles from Hard Luck, was too close.

Sick at heart, Karen willed herself to forget the night with Matt. Before she knew it, she'd be back in Oakland where she belonged.

Paragon, Inc., the engineering company she worked for, had been more than generous in giving her these vacation days for Lanni's wedding, but now the time had come to prove to her boss, Mr. Sullivan, that he'd invested the company's money wisely when he promoted her. She'd throw herself into the job, and she'd forget Matt once and for all.

Her heart ached at the thought of him. She did wish him well. Contrary to what he might believe, she wanted him to succeed. She just didn't think he would. If Matt was anything like her father, and he was, he'd find some way to sabotage himself. Only she refused to be like her mother, refused to stick around and pick up the pieces. She'd gotten out while she could and was determined to make a better life for herself.

To be on the safe side, Karen decided to curtail any contact with his family. It would be difficult, though. Karen loved Matt's parents as much as she did her own. They were generous, caring, loving people, and Lanni was like the sister she'd never had.

If this wedding had taught Karen anything, it was that she'd never get Matt out of her head, or out of her life, if she clung to his family.

The decision made, she swallowed her disappointment and decided to make more of an effort to meet new people once she got back to California. It was time. Past time. Matthew Caldwell wasn't the only attractive man in the world.

"YOU'RE LOOKING a little down in the dumps," Ben Hamilton, owner of the Hard Luck Café, said as he automatically filled Matt's coffee mug.

"What do you expect the day after a wedding?" Matt returned, fending off Ben's inquisitiveness. Matt hadn't come to socialize, but to escape.

His parents had been full of questions after seeing Karen parade barefoot up the stairs in the dress she'd worn to the wedding. It was all too clear where she'd spent the night.

"I must say your sister made a mighty pretty bride," Ben said casually.

Matt cupped the thick ceramic mug with both hands. "Thanks."

"Two weddings in Hard Luck within the space of a year. Now that's something."

Matt merely grunted in reply.

"Mitch and Bethany set their wedding date for this summer," Ben added conversationally.

Mitch Harris, the public-safety Officer—usually described as "the law around here"—and teacher Bethany Ross had announced their engagement earlier in the winter. Leave it to Matt to settle in a community where Cupid had run amuck. While he was divorced and miserable, everyone around him was stumbling all over themselves, falling in love. Not Matt. Once was enough for him, and damn it all, he loved Karen. Truly loved her.

"Bethany and Mitch's wedding's going to take place in San Francisco, but we're throwing a big reception for them when they come back from their honeymoon."

San Francisco was across the bay from Oakland. Karen lived in Oakland.

Karen. Karen. Karen.

No matter what he said or did, everything seemed to point back to Karen. At this rate he'd never be free of her.

Was that what he wanted, though?

Ben wiped the perfectly clean counter with slow, methodical strokes, patiently waiting for Matt to confide in him. Matt was well aware that a lot of the men in Hard Luck used Ben Hamilton as a sounding board. He was the kind of guy who made it easy to talk about one's troubles, but Matt wasn't interested. But then, he wasn't in the mood to talk to anyone. About anything.

He was half tempted to take his coffee and move to one of the tables. He might have, if Duke Porter hadn't chosen that moment to walk into the café. The bush pilot sidled up to the stool next to his and sat down.

Matt glared at the other man.

Duke glared back. "What's your problem?"

It was unreasonable and irrational to take his frustration out on Duke just because he'd had the gall to dance with Karen. "I've got woman troubles."

Duke snorted. "Me, too."

"You?" Ben poured a cup of coffee for the pilot and set it on the counter. "What're you talking about?"

"Well, not me personally. It's that attorney again. Tracy Santiago." His eyes narrowed as he mentioned the lawyer Mariah Douglas's family had hired to investigate Hard Luck after the town started advertising for women. Their daughter, Mariah, was the Midnight Sons secretary. "She's looking to stir up trouble. Mariah got a phone call from her on Friday. Christian told me the Santiago woman's threatening to fly up here again—probably in a couple of months—to check everything out."

"That's Christian and Sawyer's problem, isn't it?"

"Yes," Duke agreed, "but it makes me mad, you know? The way that woman keeps butting her nose into everyone's business. Here the O'Halloran brothers've done everything on the up and up—giving women jobs and housing—and what do those poor guys get in return? Hassles from some troublemaker who's accusing them of exploiting women and... and..."

"She's not your worry," Ben reminded him.

Duke didn't respond. "What's eating you?" he asked Matt, instead.

Matt wasn't keen on discussing his ex-wife, especially with Duke.

Duke didn't wait for Matt to answer him. "I imagine it's got something to do with Karen. What's with you two, anyway? The entire time she was dancing with me, Karen was asking about you."

"Me?" From the way she'd behaved, Matt had assumed he was the farthest thing from her mind.

"Oh, she tried to be subtle about it, you know, but I could see through her questions. She wanted to know about the lodge and what I thought of your plan. I told her it was a damn good one."

Matt was grateful. "I appreciate that."

"So, what's going on with you and your ex?" Duke asked again.

Matt frowned. He wasn't accustomed to discussing his personal business with anyone, not even his family. He certainly had no intention of confiding in a casual acquaintance. "We're divorced. What else do you need to know?"

"It's pretty damn obvious that you're still in love. I don't know what it is with couples these days," Duke complained to Ben. "Can anyone tell me why people who care about each other decide to call it quits? It just doesn't make sense."

Matt would've liked to argue the point, but he couldn't come up with a single, solitary thing to say. There was only one thought in his mind—what happened last night had proved beyond a doubt that he still loved Karen.

He leapt off the stool. Duke was right; instead of sitting here bemoaning his fate, he should confront Karen. She loved him. She must. Otherwise she'd never have gone to bed with him.

All she needed was a little reassurance. Okay, he'd made a few errors in judgment, but that was behind them now. The lodge was their future, and if she'd give him another chance he'd prove he could make a go of it. If she needed stability, he'd give it to her.

Matt was going after her. When he found her, he'd convince her they'd both be fools to throw away the love they shared.

He was tired of pretending he didn't care, tired of pretending he didn't miss her. His life was on course now, and once she was back everything would be perfect.

All he had to do now was explain that to Karen.

"Has she left yet?" he demanded of Duke.

"Karen?" Duke asked.

"Who the hell else do you think I'm asking about?"

Duke checked his watch. "My guess is John's about to take off. You'd better hurry if you want to catch her."

Matt didn't need any further incentive. He slapped some money down on the counter, grabbed his coat and flew out the door. The mobile unit that housed the Midnight Sons office was close by, and he sprinted the distance.

He saw John Henderson heading in the same direction, and noticed the Baron 55 sitting on the gravel runway, ready to depart for the flight to Fairbanks.

Both men reached the door to the office at the same time. "I need a few minutes alone with Karen," Matt said. He blocked John's way.

The pilot began to complain bitterly about messing up his plans, but Matt didn't care. "Listen." Matt pulled a five-dollar bill out of his pocket. "Go have a cup of Ben's coffee and give me ten minutes alone with Karen. That's all I'm asking."

John stared at the money, then scratched the side of his head. "All right, all right, just be quick, will you? I'm on a schedule." He turned away mumbling, waving away Matt's profuse thanks. "Ten minutes," he called over his shoulder. "Not a second more."

Matt waited until he'd composed his thoughts before walking inside to confront his ex-wife. Karen sat on a worn vinyl couch, staring at the floor. She glanced up when he stepped into the waiting area, and her eyes widened dramatically when she saw who it was.

"What are you doing here?" she demanded, jerking herself upright. She shrank back from him, almost as if she was afraid.

"We need to talk," he said gently.

"No, we don't. Everything's already been said. It's over. It was over a long time ago."

"Last night says otherwise."

She shook her head. "Last night was a big mistake. Please, Matt, just let me go. I don't want to talk about what happened. It didn't change anything."

"I think it did." He eased his way toward her. Pulling out a chair, he twisted it around and straddled it. "I'd been thinking about buying the lodge for a while. I saw it shortly after the fire; and I'd forgotten about it till Lanni came up here. I finally made a deal with the O'Halloran brothers. I've spent nine months now, working fifteen-hour days, doing my damnedest to have it ready for the summer tourist trade."

"Matt, listen—"

"Let me finish," he pleaded. "The reason I'm telling you about the lodge is because I consider it our future."

Karen squeezed her eyes shut.

"I realize you've heard those words before, but this time it's true. This isn't just another one of my ideas. I sank the entire trust fund my grandmother left me into this venture. I'm so far out on a limb I could pick fruit. I'm giving this my best shot, Karen. I'm risking everything for us."

"There is no us," she reminded him in a whisper.

"But there *should* be! If last night proved anything, it's that we belong together. We always have. Come back to me, Karen. You want promises? I'll give you promises. You want reassurances? Fine, you've got them. Everything will be different. We'll start over again—"

Tears rolled down her face as Karen leaned forward and brought her fingers to his mouth, silencing him. "Don't. Please, don't." She pressed her lips tightly together and swiped at the tears, then continued. "You want me to give up my job and come back here, right?"

He nodded. Of course he wanted her back here—as his wife. He wanted them to work together to build their marriage and their business. He needed her, wanted her, loved her. That had never changed.

"I've heard all this before. My mother heard it from my father, too. She loved him. She believed him every time, and he led her down one garden path after another."

"Karen, I'm not your father."

She looked away. "I'm not my mother, either. I can't— I won't do what you're asking. My future is with Paragon. My home isn't in Alaska anymore, it's in Oakland. Don't you realize how many times you've said almost those identical words to me? Six months from now, you'll be bored again and you'll have some other wonderful dream to follow. I can't live that way. I tried. I honestly tried."

"But—"

"Matt, stop, please. The bottom line is that I'm not willing to throw my career down the drain for another one of your madcap schemes, no matter how promising it sounds."

Matt stood, his mind racing frantically as he tried to find a way of convincing her to stay.

"I have my own life now," she said. "I won't give up everything I've worked to achieve. Not for your dreams. Because for the first time in years, Matt, I have dreams of my own."

He was fighting a losing battle and he knew it.

"I'm going to find a man with a steady job and a savings account. I'm going to settle down in a house with a white picket fence and raise a passel of children." A sob shook her shoulders. "And I'm going to do everything I can to put our marriage behind me.'' Having said that, she reached for her suitcase and rushed out the door.

"MOM!" TEN-YEAR-OLD Scott O'Halloran burst in the front door with Eagle Catcher, his husky and faithful friend, trotting behind him.

Abbey looked up from the magazine she was reading.

"Sawyer—I mean Dad—let me fly his plane this afternoon," her son announced proudly.

Abbey's gaze instantly connected with that of her husband as he followed her son into the house.

"I didn't actually fly the plane," Scott quickly amended, "but Sawyer let me hold the control stick, and he told me all about the different instruments on the panel."

"It's time, honey," Sawyer said, kissing her on the cheek.

Abbey wasn't convinced of that. "But, Sawyer, he's only ten."

"Aw, Mom, you gotta stop treating me like a little kid."

Abbey swallowed a laugh. She recalled the day she'd arrived in Hard Luck with her two children in tow. She'd been one of the first women lured to town with the promise of a job, a house and land. She'd come hoping to make a new life for herself and her children.

The last thing either she or Sawyer had been looking for was love. But they'd found it, with each other. They must have had the fastest courtship in Hard Luck's history, Abbey mused. In retrospect, she wouldn't change a thing. Not only was she deeply in love with her husband, but Sawyer had legally adopted Scott and Susan, and he worked hard at being a good father.

"My dad was teaching me the basic elements of flying when I was ten," he assured her. "Trust me, I'm not going to do anything to put either of us in danger."

Abbey knew that went without saying; nevertheless, she couldn't help worrying.

"I'm going to find Ronny Gold," Scott told them. "I'll be back before dinner." He was out the door with another burst of speed. The silver-eyed husky raced along at his side.

"I wonder what Charles and Lanni are up to about now," Sawyer said with a cocky grin.

"They're probably lying on a sandy beach soaking up the sunshine."

Sawyer sat next to her on the sofa. "Remember our honeymoon?"

Abbey smiled. They hadn't actually seen too much of Hawaii.

"If you recall, we didn't spend a lot of time on any of those beaches. As far as I was concerned, all we needed was a bed and a little privacy."

"Sawyer!"

"I'm crazy about you, woman."

"Good thing, because I'm crazy about you, too." She turned, sliding her arms around his waist. The happiness she'd found with him continued to astound her. When she'd least expected it, Sawyer had given her back her heart, given her a second chance at love.

"Don't worry about cooking tonight," he said. "I thought I'd treat us all to dinner."

"On a Monday night?"

"Sure." He grinned. "Ben's started a frequent-eater program, and—"

"A *what?*"

"You know, like the airlines' frequent-flyer clubs."

"Oh. Of course."

"He's trying to drum up a little business, and I thought we should support his creativity."

Abbey gave Sawyer a quick kiss. "And have some of Ben's apple pie in the bargain."

"Then, later," Sawyer said, cozying up to her, "I thought you and I could relive some of those wonderful moments from our own honeymoon."

Abbey had a feeling he wasn't talking about lazing around the beach, either.

KAREN HAD NEVER felt worse, emotionally or physically. Bad enough to make a doctor's appointment.

Spring was generally one of her favorite times of year. The changes in the California weather weren't as dramatic as those in Alaska, but the heavy Oakland air seemed to hold less smog.

She'd been living in California for several months now, and she wondered if she'd ever grow accustomed to looking at the horizon and seeing nothing but a brown haze.

She'd hoped to adjust more quickly to life in California, but so far she hadn't. True, there were compensations—a staggering variety of stores and restaurants, lots of TV channels, consistently moderate weather. But daylight in the winter months had taken some getting used to. Freeways continued to unnerve her. Traffic intimidated her. And so many people! It boggled her mind. The contrast between California and Alaska was never more striking than on the freeways.

Karen had made friends. All female. It might have helped if she'd been able to get involved in another relationship. But she wasn't ready, and she didn't know how long it would be before she was.

Still, no matter how many months or years it took, she was determined to forget Matt.

First, though, she had to get over this strange malady of hers. A woman friend in her office had recommended Dr

Perry, and if the patients filling his waiting room were any indication, he must be good.

She flipped through a glossy women's magazine as she waited for the nurse to call her name. Checking her watch, she saw that it was already twenty minutes past her appointment time. Actually Karen didn't mind the wait because she didn't know what she'd say once she saw him. She didn't have any real symptoms. She just felt...bad. She slept more than she should. Her appetite was nonexistent. And she cried at the drop of a hat. Just the other night she found herself weeping over a television advertisement for a camera. A camera, for heaven's sake!

Her real fear was that Dr. Perry would announce she suffered all the symptoms of someone chronically depressed and tell her she should make an appointment with a mental-health professional. She was prepared to do that if he suggested it.

When her name was finally called, she followed the nurse to the cubicle and sat on a molded plastic chair. Considering what this appointment was costing her, she'd think Dr. Perry could at least afford a decent chair.

The nurse, Mrs. Webster, according to her nameplate, read over the questionnaire Karen had completed earlier. "It says here you haven't been feeling well."

"Yes," Karen responded crisply. "I think it might be the smog."

"The smog." Mrs. Webster made a notation on the chart.

"You see, I'm from Alaska. I've never been exposed to smog before. My lungs don't like it."

"I don't imagine they do."

"Personally I believe it's affecting my general health. I just feel crummy." Although she felt fine at the moment,

Karen found herself battling back tears. "And I—I seem to have developed the ability to weep at nothing."

Mrs. Webster's eyes searched out hers. "Oh?"

Karen fumbled in her purse for a tissue and blew her nose. "I tear up at the most ridiculous things. I can't tell you how embarrassing it is."

"You miss Alaska?"

"Yes...no. I don't want to go back...I mean I do, I really do, but I can't. You see, I accepted this promotion, and Paragon, Inc., the company I work for, moved me here." She stopped and blew her nose a second time. "Sorry."

"Let's go back to the part about feeling crummy. Do you have any other symptoms the doctor should know about?"

She shrugged. "Not really."

Mrs. Webster walked over to the drawer and took out some medical instruments. "I'm sure Dr. Perry's going to want to get a blood sample from you."

"Fine." She held out her arm for the nurse. "I feel sluggish. That's one of my symptoms," she clarified. "I wake up in the morning and I don't want to get out of bed."

"I'll mention that to the doctor."

"Do you think it might be the smog?" she asked hopefully, watching the older woman.

"I don't know. I'll let the doctor decide. But we've recently seen several people with low-grade flu symptoms."

That was reassuring. Maybe all she had was a simple case of the flu.

Ten minutes later, after the nurse had taken some blood and Karen had changed out of her clothes and into a flimsy paper gown, she met Dr. Perry. He was much younger than she'd expected. Maybe thirty, if that.

"Hello, Karen," he said. His voice was kindly.

"Hi." She felt more than a little ridiculous in her blue paper outfit.

While she tucked the gown more securely over her thighs, Dr. Perry read her chart. "I understand you haven't been feeling much like your usual self lately."

"No, not at all. I think it must be the smog."

"Tired. Sluggish. Weepy."

"That about sums it up."

He glanced up from the chart and held her gaze.

"Mrs. Webster said there's been a low-grade flu going around," she suggested.

"Yes," Dr. Perry agreed, "but this sounds like something else. Tell me, Karen, is there any possibility you could be pregnant?"

CHAPTER THREE

MATT STOOD in the main room of the lodge and handed Lanni the glossy brochure he'd produced. He studied her closely, eager for his sister's response. Since Lanni was a writer, he'd gone to her for advice about the text and even the design. Now the brochure was ready to mail out.

"Matt, this is really great!"

"Yeah, it looks good, but does it make you want to spend several thousand dollars to fly to northern Alaska?"

"Sure," she said.

Matt remained unconvinced. "What about the section on dogsledding?"

"I think it's a good idea." But her enthusiasm sounded forced, and when she hesitated, Matt wondered if she'd be honest or just tell him what she thought he wanted to hear.

"Do you really believe people want to learn how to run a dog team?" she asked after an awkward moment.

"Positive. It's the in thing. Men, and plenty of women, too, are looking for more than relaxation when they take their vacations." He strived to keep his voice calm and matter-of-fact. "They want adventure. Sure, lazing on a beach might sound good, but after two or three days most folks with A-type personalities are bored to tears. The people who can afford this kind of pricy vacation are generally professional people who're driven to succeed. Always looking for new challenges. I'm offering them something unique."

Lanni grinned. "I'll say. But city folks aren't going to know how to harness dogs or hitch them to a sled."

"That's where the mushers come in, and I've got the real McCoy." Matt was thrilled with the response he'd gotten from the professional mushers. "Anyone who signs on is going to learn it all. That's part of the thrill."

"I hope this works." But it was plain Lanni remained skeptical.

"My gut instinct tells me this is going to catch on big."

Matt sincerely hoped he was right. The survival of the business depended on his ability to convince travel agents across the United States to book their clients into Hard Luck Lodge. His vacation packages included guided fishing tours during the summer months and dogsledding in the winter.

"Imagine taking a hundred-mile trek above the Arctic Circle, driving your own team of dogs," Matt said, struggling to control his excitement. He figured if he could convince his sister, then he could sell this package to just about anyone. "I've got everything spelled out right here," he said, pointing to the listing of six- and eight-day trips between February and April.

"Several of my guides have run the Iditarod themselves. They know all there is to know about dogs and sledding. This venture helps them, too. The mushers can use the money, and I've been more than fair in giving them a cut of the action."

Lanni's attention returned to the brochure. "I like the way you mention the history of the Iditarod. 'In January 1925, Leonhard Seppala, a Norwegian musher,'" she read aloud, "'rushed diphtheria serum 675 miles from the end of the Alaska Railroad to Nome. The trip took just over five days.'"

"Even now the Iditarod is called the most rugged race on earth." Matt wasn't telling Lanni anything she didn't already know. "People dream about this kind of adventure."

"Then it's that thrill-seeking vacationer you're hoping to attract?"

"Exactly." Matt wanted this venture to succeed for more reasons than he cared to contemplate. He had something to prove to himself—and to Karen. "But it'll appeal to lots of other people, too.

"I'm listed with the Airline Report Corporation now," he said, although he suspected his sister didn't fully understand the significance of this. It meant that Hard Luck Lodge was formally listed with professional travel agents around the country. If a client came in looking for a place to fish, he or she would learn about the lodge.

"Good."

"I'm mailing out literally thousands of the brochures and offering plenty of incentives to agents to book their clients."

"Incentives? Like what?"

"Well, for one thing," he said, "the first ten agents who call me with reservations will receive a two-night fishing package."

"That's a great idea."

"I thought so." He leaned against the registration counter, crossing his arms, and surveyed the room. A gentle fire flickered in the massive stone fireplace. What the room really needed was those little touches a woman gave a home. He'd wanted to ask Lanni, but she'd already helped with the brochure; besides, she and Charles were newlyweds and he didn't want to intrude in their lives.

Karen had always been great with that sort of thing. It amazed him the way she could turn a dinky apartment into a real home, with the colors she used and plants and the placement of a few carefully chosen things. She had a gift for making a room look inviting.

"Now tell me about this trip you're taking," Lanni said, breaking into his thoughts. Actually he was grateful. He didn't want to think about Karen. She'd made her position clear—she didn't want him in her life—and he was determined to accept that.

"It's a ten-city West Coast tour to meet personally with travel agents," he explained. "I'll be giving a presentation in each city, along with other lodge owners. That way, the agents can ask me any questions they have."

Lanni nudged him playfully. "One thing's for sure, no one else is going to offer dogsledding."

"Probably not," Matt agreed.

Lanni glanced over his travel itinerary and slowly raised her eyes to connect with his. "You'll be in Oakland."

"Yeah." He didn't pretend not to know what that meant. Karen lived in Oakland. Well, he'd made up his mind a long time ago that he wasn't going to see her.

A man had his pride, and she'd trampled his for the last time. Despite their night together, she wasn't interested in a reconciliation; fine, then that was the way things would be.

"I mailed Karen one of your brochures."

Matt stifled a groan. This was the problem with Lanni and Karen's being such good friends. A part of him wanted Karen to see the brochure because he was damn proud of it. Proud of everything he'd accomplished in less than a year. But at the same time he didn't want to hear her tell him that his venture was another—what had she called it?—madcap scheme. Contrary to what his ex-wife felt, buying the lodge wasn't a passing fancy.

"Don't you want to know what Karen said?" Lanni asked.

"No," he lied. "She's out of my life now."

"But you still care about her."

Matt wasn't about to let his sister meddle in his life. "Stay out of it, Lanni. What's happened between Karen and me is none of your business."

"Don't be so quick to shut me out, big brother," his sister said, making her eyes wide and innocent, "As I remember, *you* tried to interfere in my relationship with Charles. You manipulated us into meeting so we'd settle our differences."

"As I remember," he echoed, "you didn't appreciate my interference. Karen and I won't, either. I love you, Lanni, but I want you to stay out of this."

Lanni suddenly looked uncomfortable.

"What did you do?" Matt demanded.

"I...I wrote and told her you were going to be in Oakland."

That wouldn't make the least bit of difference, Matt figured. "She won't look me up, and I'm certainly not going out of my way to see her, if that's what you're thinking." And he wouldn't. Karen wanted nothing more to do with him.

Fine. Great. He'd adjust. It wasn't like this was earth-shattering news. He'd been a little slow to get the message; he should have taken the hint when she filed for divorce.

"Whether or not you see her is up to you," Lanni assured him softly, almost as if she was aware that she'd risked offending him, "but I gave Karen the name of your hotel."

The anger caused him to clench his fists. He didn't want *anyone* interfering in his life, least of all his kid sister. Irritated though he was, he understood that her intentions were good. Lanni and Charles were so much in love themselves, it influenced the way they looked at everyone else's life.

"Don't be angry with me," she pleaded.

Matt said nothing.

"Remember, I'm the one who volunteered to take reservations when you're down in the lower forty-eight rounding up business."

It could be wishful thinking on his part, but Matt hoped this tour would generate enough interest in Hard Luck Lodge that bookings would immediately start pouring in. Lanni had offered to run the office while he was away. Actually the arrangement suited them both, since she needed a quiet place to write.

His sister left soon afterward, and Matt wandered into the kitchen with its gleaming new appliances. He was eager for paying guests. Eager to host tourists from all over the world.

So far, he'd managed to acquire only a handful of reservations. His listing in the ARC had been entered late—too late to attract much of the lucrative fishing business. He had a lot to learn about attracting tourists, but he was willing and able. And determined. He would make a go of this lodge or die trying.

"MATT HAS A RIGHT to know about the baby." Lanni's voice sounded tinny on Karen's telephone line. "You don't know how close I came to telling him myself this afternoon."

"But you didn't, did you?" Karen cried in alarm. If anyone told her ex-husband she was two months pregnant, it should be her. Except that it was turning out to be even harder than she'd thought.

"No, I didn't," Lanni assured her. "Listen, Karen, if you don't want to tell him face-to-face, why don't you write him a letter?"

"I can't." After the things she'd said to him, she wouldn't blame him if he returned her letter unopened. Besides, this was the kind of news that was better given in person.

"You should have called him right away." The censure in Lanni's voice was strong. It might have been a mistake to confide in her ex-sister-in-law, but Karen had had to tell *someone*.

"You've already waited a month longer than you should have," Lanni reminded her.

Karen had no defense. "I know."

"But you have the chance to rectify it all now. He's going to be in Oakland on Friday."

Karen bit her lower lip. "So you said."

The pause lasted long enough for Karen to wonder if Lanni was still on the line. When she spoke again, her voice was gentle. "How are you feeling?"

Karen rested her hand on her abdomen. "Better." No one had warned her how dreadful morning sickness could be. The first few weeks of the pregnancy she'd suffered few such symptoms, but now...

At the time of her original doctor's appointment she'd felt tired and restless and rather depressed. But that had changed dramatically after the first month. She wasn't depressed anymore—but not a day passed when she didn't view parts of a toilet that were never meant to be seen at such close range.

Despite the past month's discomforts, Karen was thrilled to be pregnant. She'd always wanted children but hadn't started a family with Matt because she'd wanted him to settle into a permanent job first; but he'd always dragged his feet. Furthermore, he'd seemed reluctant to have a child, and that was one reason she'd delayed telling her ex-husband he was about to become a father.

To some women this pregnancy would have been a disaster, but Karen couldn't help being excited. She wanted this child. Despite everything, she loved Matt. And as far as their relationship was concerned, the baby would be an additional complication to an already complicated situation.

"I hope you'll reconsider," Lanni said, and Karen realized she hadn't been listening.

"Reconsider?"

"Going to see Matt. You should, if for no other reason than to view his presentation. He had Charles and me sit through it before he left, and I have to tell you, Karen, I was impressed."

"He's talking to travel agents?"

"That's right. He's put together this wonderful slide show. I was so busy this winter finishing up my commitments to the newspaper in Anchorage that I didn't pay a lot of attention to what Matt was doing. Did you know he spent ten days on the tundra with nothing more than a tent and a team of sled dogs?"

"Matt?"

"He told me he couldn't very well sell the adventure if he hadn't experienced it himself. I couldn't believe his pictures. They're fabulous."

Karen could easily imagine Matt standing in front of an audience. He was good with people, outgoing, friendly. And a persuasive kind of guy.

"When he talked about the dogs," Lanni went on, "his eyes just sparkled with excitement. If the number of phone calls I'm getting here is any indication, he's doing a good job of selling the winter packages."

"You mean to say he's actually convinced people to visit the Arctic in winter?" Karen had trouble believing it, but then, what did she know about vacations? In the entire four years of their married life, they hadn't been able to afford even one.

"I've taken at least ten reservations, and Matt's only been gone a week," Lanni announced proudly. "More are coming in every day."

"Lanni, please don't tell me he's actually planning to guide a group of innocent tourists himself. With a pack of highly excitable dogs, no less."

"Of course not," Lanni answered with a short laugh. "He's hired professional mushers."

"Oh." Karen felt ridiculous for having asked.

"Are you going to see him or not?"

"I . . . don't know yet."

"Well, you'd better decide soon because he'll only be in Oakland one night. He's scheduled to go to—" Karen heard a rustle of papers "—Portland, Seattle and then home."

"I'm not making any promises," Karen said, but she knew Lanni was right. Matt deserved to know that he would be a father in seven months. She just didn't know how he'd react to the news.

MATT SAW KAREN the moment she slipped into the back row of the meeting room. Even from this distance, the first thing he noticed was how pale she looked. He sat on the stage with a number of other lodge operators, all working hard to sell their tour packages. Luckily he'd already given his presentation, so the pressure was off and he could study his ex-wife.

She'd lost weight, and he wondered if that was intentional. If so, she was too thin, but she wouldn't appreciate hearing that from him.

The temptation to walk off the stage and confront her then and there was almost overwhelming. He might have done it if not for their last conversation.

Well, this time, damn it, she could come to him. He was tired of having his teeth shoved down his throat every time he attempted to reason with her.

Then again, maybe she didn't intend to seek him out. Maybe she was only here to satisfy her curiosity. Or because she'd promised Lanni. Fine, so be it, he decided. With effort he managed to keep his eyes resolutely trained on the current speaker. But again and again, his gaze drifted back to her, and he experienced a twinge of regret.

The moderator walked to the microphone. "Are there any questions?"

A hand went up in the middle of the room. "I have one for Mr. Caldwell."

Matt stood.

"Do you have any response to the animal-rights people who question using dogs to pull sleds?"

Matt had gotten the same question in almost every city. First, I want to assure you that the dogs are loved and cared for the way most people look after their own children. As for the rigors of life on the trail, the huskies are thoroughly happy. Running was what they were born to, and they love it. Their comfort range is amazing. Until the weather drops to around thirty below, many sled dogs don't even care to sleep in a kennel."

"Are the dogs dangerous?" someone called out.

"No way," Matt said, smiling. "Mostly they're playful and fun. At rest stops along the winter trails they cool down by rolling in the snow. For the first mile of a run, they're excited and excitable, but even then an inexperienced musher can learn to manage them. After the first day or so, everyone will come to know the dogs by name and personality.''

Since he offered something new and interesting, Matt fielded the majority of the questions. As with his audiences in other cities, he felt he'd accomplished his purpose. The travel agents certainly seemed enthusiastic. But even as he was speaking, his gaze was drawn back to Karen. Pride be damned. He wasn't letting her off the hook so easily. If she wanted to walk out, fine, but he made sure she knew he'd seen her.

Following the question-and-answer session, the applause was vigorous. Matt gathered his notes, glancing up only once to see if he could find Karen. His heart fell when he realized she was nowhere in sight.

Then, when he was convinced she'd run away like a frightened rabbit, he turned around and found her standing no more than a foot away.

At close range, she looked paler than she had from the other end of the room. His concern was immediate.

"Karen, have you been ill?"

"No. Well, you wouldn't call it ill."

The woman spoke in riddles.

"Matt, do you have time for a drink?"

She was actually inviting him. That was progress. He glanced at his watch, wanting her to sweat it out. "I suppose." He tried to make it sound as if he was squeezing her in between appointments.

Carrying his briefcase, he led the way to the hotel's cocktail lounge and ordered two glasses of white wine.

"No, just one glass," Karen said to the waitress. "I'll have an herbal tea. Any kind."

Matt looked at her in astonishment. "Tea? I thought you liked wine."

"I'm avoiding alcohol," she explained, keeping her gaze averted.

He couldn't imagine why, and he wasn't going to ask. She was the one with the agenda here, and frankly he was more than a little curious about what she wanted to say.

"I was impressed with your answers to the questions," she began. "I'd hoped to be here for your presentation, but... I wasn't feeling well earlier," she began, sounding shaky and uncertain. She rallied and continued, "Karen mailed me one of your brochures. They look terrific."

"Thanks." He was coldly determined not to make this easy for her. Not after the grief she'd given him, the pain she'd caused.

"She told me you've been getting a number of reservations since you went on tour."

"So I understand."

Their drinks arrived and Matt signed the bill with his room number. He noticed that when Karen sipped her tea, her hand trembled. Now he was beginning to get worried.

"Karen, what did you mean earlier about being sick?"

"I'm not sick."

"Oh, yeah, I can tell. How much weight have you lost?" He hadn't intended to be sarcastic, but he hated cat-and-mouse games. If she had something to say, he'd prefer she just spit it out.

He waited for her answer, determined not to speak again until she'd said something relevant; she remained silent. His resolve lasted all of one minute.

"How's the career coming?" he asked, hoping she noticed his choice of words. She'd worked for the engineering firm for three years. She was an employer's dream—conscientious, organized, efficient. It hadn't surprised him that when her boss was promoted he'd made her his executive assistant and moved her to California with him.

"Great."

Somehow Matt didn't believe her.

"Mr. Sullivan giving you problems?" he asked. In some ways, the older man was more like a father to Karen than her own. Matt couldn't imagine Sullivan creating difficulties for her.

"Actually he's been very understanding about the amount of time I've missed from work."

"Missed work?" That didn't sound like Karen, either. In the four years of their marriage, he couldn't recall her taking a single day of sick leave.

"I've been having some trouble...mostly in the mornings." She leveled her gaze at him, as though she expected him to make some logical deduction from that bit of information.

"Ah, you've got PMS," he said, attempting a small joke.

From the disapproving glare she sent him, he gathered she didn't find it humorous. "Matt, you can really be obtuse."

"Me? Listen, Karen, you're the one who wouldn't allow me to finish our last conversation. As far as I'm concerned, if you've got something to say, just say it, because I've got a flight to catch in the morning."

Lifting her chin to a dignified angle, she reached for her purse and stood. "You're absolutely right," she said in a clear voice. "I've been beating around the bush." Her purse strap slipped off her shoulder and she quickly secured it. "I don't have a perpetual case of PMS, Matt, as amusing as you appear to find that. The reason I've lost weight can be attributed to something else. I have what's known as morning sickness. Now, if you'll excuse me, I'll leave you to mull that one over." She turned abruptly and walked out of the lounge.

"Morning sickness," Matt repeated, and downed the last of his wine in one swallow. The words echoed in his brain and his gaze flew to her retreating figure. He bolted upright. "You're pregnant?"

Karen turned the corner and was gone.

"She's pregnant," Matt shouted to the cocktail waitress. Then, before he completely lost Karen, he raced to the lobby in enough time to see her walking out the front doors.

"Karen, wait!"

Either she didn't hear him or she was determined to ignore him. It was just like her to drop that kind of bombshell and then leave him to deal with the shrapnel all on his own.

He didn't catch up with her until she'd reached her car.

"What the hell do you mean you're pregnant?" he demanded. "How did something like this happen?"

She turned around and glared at him.

"Weren't you on the pill?"

"Why should I be?" she asked. "We were divorced, remember?"

As if he'd forgotten that!

"Don't you dare suggest birth control is entirely up to the woman," she said between gritted teeth.

Matt was having trouble taking all this in. "But how?"

"Well," she muttered sarcastically, "here's what I remember from biology class. The woman provides the egg and the man supplies the sperm."

"I know all that!" he snapped. "What I'm talking about is us. We're both responsible adults. I can't believe we didn't consider the possibility of your getting pregnant." He pushed the hair away from his face and leaned against the side of her car. His legs felt like gelatin.

"It might have helped if you'd broken the news a bit more gently," he accused.

"It would help if you weren't looking for someone to blame."

"That's not true," he flared. He rubbed his hand along the back of his neck. "You're going to need financial help." Since his budget was tight, money was the first thing that came to mind.

Karen made a growling sound, and he looked up to find her glaring at him again, her eyes bright with unshed tears. "You're impossible!" she shouted.

"What did I say now?"

"Nothing." She shook her head. "I've fulfilled my obligation. I told you about the baby. I do apologize for any inconvenience this might cause you." Sarcasm dripped from every word. "Perhaps the best alternative is to have my attorney talk to your attorney. Goodbye, Matt."

With that, she unlocked her car door and climbed in.

"You can't leave," he shouted as she started the car's engine. "We have to talk." But she ignored him as if he hadn't even spoken. "Karen, damn it, would you listen to me?"

She twisted around to look over her shoulder before shoving the car into reverse. Then she backed out of the space and drove off, leaving him standing in the middle of the parking lot, seething with frustration.

KAREN BARELY SLEPT that night. She wasn't sure what she'd expected from Matt, but not the sarcastic arrogance he'd dished up and served her while they were in the cocktail lounge. He'd seemed to take delight in her discomfort.

When she'd finally garnered enough courage to tell him about the pregnancy, he'd reacted as if she'd plotted against him. As if it was important to somehow assign blame for the unexpected pregnancy.

What really bothered her, Karen decided, sometime in the wee hours of the morning, was the fact that his reaction was completely contrary to the romantic picture she'd painted in her mind. For weeks she'd envisioned telling Matt about their baby and watching his eyes go all soft as he regarded her with tenderness and love.

After being married to Matt for four years, she should've known better. The man didn't possess a romantic bone in his body. Furthermore, why should he be excited and pleased because she was pregnant? *He'd* never wanted a baby.

He didn't want a child now any more than he had when they were married. A baby was an inconvenience. A baby got in the way of his plans.

She'd listened to his arguments about financial security often enough to know exactly what he'd been thinking. If Matthew Caldwell lived to be a hundred, he'd never be financially secure—simply because he'd never hold a job long enough to make it possible.

She was better off without him. On a conscious level she knew that, but on an emotional one, it hurt. Damn it, it really hurt. If ever there was a time in her life she needed coddling and comfort, it was now.

Although the doctors assured her the morning sickness would lessen with time, she hadn't seen any evidence of it. The following morning, like every other morning for weeks, she rose, managed to down a simple breakfast of tea and soda crackers and promptly lost it. Spending most of the night stewing about Matt hadn't helped her physical condition.

By nine she was stretched out on the sofa with a blanket. She'd placed a bucket on the floor beside her because of the queasiness in her stomach.

The doorbell chimed, but she was in no mood for company, and ignored it.

"Damn it, Karen! Open the door."

Matt.

"Leave me alone," she shouted, draining what little energy she had left.

Disregarding her demand, Matt opened the door himself and stepped into her small apartment. She never had learned to keep her door locked. Unfortunately the habit had followed her to California.

Matt looked as pale as she had the night before. He wore the same clothes he'd had on then. If she was guessing, she'd say he hadn't been to bed.

He lowered himself into the chair across from her, and his gaze fell on the bucket.

"No one told me getting pregnant was like suffering the worst case of flu known to womankind," she muttered. She sipped flat soda pop through a straw.

"Is it always like this?"

"Every morning for the past four weeks. And the occasional evening."

He frowned, and although he didn't say anything his look was apologetic. "That's the reason you've missed so much work?"

She nodded. "Listen," she said, rallying somewhat, "I'm sorry for hitting you with the news. Lanni's been telling me for weeks that you had a right to know. I—"

"Lanni knows?"

Karen nodded again.

He expelled his breath loudly. "Anyone else?"

"No. I wouldn't have told her, but—"

"Never mind," he said, cutting her off. "It's not important." He leaned forward and rubbed his palms together. "I've been giving this a lot of thought. For the past twelve hours, as a matter of fact."

She stared at him, waiting.

"I want you to move up to Hard Luck with me. The sooner we can remarry the better and—"

"No," she returned adamantly. "The baby is the last reason on earth for us to remarry."

CHAPTER FOUR

"YOU WON'T REMARRY ME?" Matt had the audacity to look shocked. "What about the baby?"

Karen closed her eyes. She wasn't feeling well enough to argue with her ex-husband. The nausea seemed to be worse this morning than usual and it was difficult enough to think clearly without Matt's questions.

"Karen—"

"I'm fine." She wasn't, but explaining how awful she felt required more strength than she could muster.

His brow creased with concern. "Will you be this sick the entire pregnancy?"

"I don't know." Good heavens, she prayed that wouldn't be the case. Her doctor seemed to think the bouts of vomiting would pass after the first three months. Eight weeks into the pregnancy, and Karen had experienced no lessening of symptoms. Why they should hit her so forcefully in the second month baffled her.

"Are you able to work?"

"Yes . . . no. I've used up all my sick leave." It hurt to admit that. Her boss had been wonderfully understanding, but she knew being away from her desk days on end was a terrible inconvenience to Mr. Sullivan.

In the past four weeks, Karen had spent an average of only two to three hours a day at the office. Even when she did manage to show up, she was unable to give one hundred percent.

As if he couldn't bear to remain seated, Matt got to his feet and started pacing. "Who's your doctor? Maybe I should talk to him myself. You shouldn't be this ill. Is there something you're not telling me?"

"Like what?"

"There's no possibility this will be a multiple birth, is there?"

Twins? Triplets? Karen hadn't given the matter a thought. "Of course not," she assured him, but it made her wonder. Good grief, how could she ever manage alone with twins? Then, because he'd raised the question, she asked, "What makes you think I could be having twins?"

"I read about something like this once where the wife—the woman suffered acute bouts of morning sickness and it ended up she had quints."

"Quintuplets!" The thought horrified Karen, but when she glanced up at Matt, he was grinning from ear to ear as though the idea brought him considerable enjoyment. "Just think of all the publicity that would bring the lodge."

Naturally he'd think of his precious lodge and not her. "Wipe that smile off your face, Matthew Caldwell."

Matt sat back down and leaned forward. "This is pretty incredible, you know."

That wasn't the impression he'd given her the night before. Okay, the news had come as a shock, but he had a long way to go to play his part in her fantasy. She'd pictured him bringing her a huge bouquet of flowers and a large teddy bear. So far, all he'd brought her was a bunch of silly questions and an outrageous demand. He assumed that because she was pregnant they should remarry as soon as possible. Sweep their difficulties under the rug and pretend they didn't exist—that was Matt's way of dealing with her pregnancy.

"Think about it, Karen," he continued, cocky grin firmly back in place. "In all the years we've known each other, the night of Lanni's wedding was probably the first time we ever made love without protection."

That was the last thing she wanted to be reminded of, especially when she felt so wretched. She remained on the sofa with her head dangling over the edge to be sure her aim for the bucket was on target.

"The odds of your getting pregnant from our one and only...lapse must be astronomical."

Leave it to Matt to get egotistical over something like this. The man was marinating in his own testosterone. Men and their pride! Karen would never understand it.

"Trust me, Matt, this is not the time to gloat." The nausea worsened and she closed her eyes, fearing she was about to lose whatever was left in her stomach.

He chuckled, then seemed to realize she wasn't joking. She must have gone even paler, because he reached over and brushed the hair from her brow.

"What can I do to help?" he asked gently.

It was his tenderness that nearly did her in. Karen had to fight back tears. "Nothing," she whispered, and breathed in deeply. "It'll pass in a moment." Sometimes it did, and other times it didn't. "It might be best if you left—I don't feel up to company."

"Oh, no, you don't," Matt warned. "I'm not walking out of this apartment until you and I have made some decisions."

"We have nothing to decide."

"What about the doctor and hospital bills?"

Karen hated to admit she was hurting in the pocketbook. The medical bills were beginning to mount. The health insurance provided through Paragon, Inc., paid eighty percent, but the twenty percent she had to pay grew with each doctor's visit. She didn't need a calculator to realize that with the difficulties she'd already experienced, she would soon run into the thousands. And the fact that her attendance at work was sporadic at best didn't help her financial situation.

"Are you offering to help?" she asked stiffly. Matt had never been good with money. It used to drive her crazy the way he'd write checks without keeping a balance in their checkbook. He'd often stack up two or three months' worth of bank statements before he'd reconcile their account. He wasn't irresponsible or reckless; he just wanted to make the effort worth his while. At least, that was what he always claimed.

Karen should have realized the moment he mentioned his plans to be an accountant that the effort was doomed. He'd never been interested enough in numbers.

"The baby is my responsibility, too," he reminded her.

But it went without saying that Matt was in no position to be giving her money. Not with launching Hard Luck Lodge. He'd sunk every penny he could scrounge plus his entire inheritance in this venture. Knowing Matt the way she did, Karen doubted there was anything left.

"I know, but—"

"Karen." He clasped her hand between his and got down on his knees beside her. "It makes sense to put aside this nonsense once and for all. We belong together. We always have—now more than ever."

"Nonsense?" Did he honestly believe that the agony of their divorce had been a trivial decision on her part? Leaving Matt and filing for divorce had been the most difficult painful thing she'd ever done. For him to make light of what it had cost her emotionally proved he'd never understand her.

"Okay, so you don't want to move to Hard Luck," he said as if living in the Arctic was all that held her back.

She closed her eyes, stunned that he knew so little about her.

"Do you?" he asked hopefully.

She opened her eyes, confused by his question.

"Would you agree to marry me and move to Hard Luck?"

"Oh, Matt, please don't ask that of me. Not now when I feel this wretched."

"I want to take care of you."

He was going to have his hands full running the lodge. As for taking care of her, well, she'd been doing a fair job of that for years.

"No," she said fighting herself, as well as him. She needed him, really needed him, perhaps for the first time. Yet as hard as she tried, Karen couldn't put the past behind her. Matt had fallen short of her expectations so often. He'd made promises in the past and let her down. There was so much more at stake now.

"No," Matt echoed, his face tense. He stood and moved to the living room window, staring quietly out for several minutes. When he turned around, anger and frustration seemed to radiate from him in waves. The tightness around his mouth and eyes made his expression piercing and grim.

"I've never understood what I did that was so terrible," he said, his voice low. "Okay, I agree I fumbled around for a while looking for the right career. I knew that bothered you but, Karen, I'm not your father. You complain about my tendency to bounce from job to job, but was that really so bad? We never went hungry, the rent was paid and we had a decent life."

Karen wanted to argue that it was pure luck he found work so easily and you couldn't always count on luck. It was the uncertainty of the situation that drove her crazy. She'd fret and worry about the rent, although somehow, they'd always managed.

"I'm faithful and loyal. I never drank or abused you in any way."

"Matt, please—"

"I've always loved you. The day we stood before the judge and he pounded his gavel and solemnly proclaimed we were no longer married, I still loved you. You're carrying my child, and I love you more now than I thought possible—but I can't force you to care for me."

Karen covered her face in an effort to hold back the words that would tell him how much she cared.

"You want to shut me out of your life," he said starkly. "You want to ignore the fact that the child you're carrying is mine, too. I never thought I'd say it, but maybe you were right—having my attorney talk to yours might be the best way to handle this." Without another word, he walked to the door and left.

The sharp and sudden pain in Karen's abdomen took her by surprise. The unexpectedness of it was one thing, but the intensity of the attack took her breath away. She gasped and doubled up.

Something was very wrong.

Edges of darkness crowded her vision, and she feared she was about to faint. With what little strength she possessed, Karen heaved herself from the sofa and stumbled to the front door.

"Matt." She screamed his name, frantic now with fear. He was halfway to the parking lot when he heard her.

"Help me..." she pleaded, sobbing uncontrollably. She stretched one arm toward him and clutched her stomach with the other. "I think I'm losing the baby."

MATT SAT in the waiting area outside the emergency room at Oakland Hospital. He'd tried a dozen times in the past two hours to see Karen but had been told the doctor was still with her. Two hours!

The waiting room was packed. There were several crying, sick children, a man with a bloody towel wrapped around his hand and a young mother gently singing a lullaby to her fussing two-year-old. A couple of girls were staring at the fish in an aquarium, while two or three men seemed glued to the lone TV, which was tuned to CNN.

Matt hadn't glanced at the television or the aquarium once. He was too worried about Karen and the baby. He was afraid the length of time she'd been with the doctor didn't bode well for the pregnancy.

He closed his eyes and forced himself to concentrate on breathing. A crushing sadness lodged in his chest. He'd known about the baby less than twenty-four hours, yet he deeply grieved the loss of his son or daughter. He would never hold this baby in his arms, never change a diaper or hear his child's first word.

Glancing toward the swinging doors, Matt willed someone—anyone—to come and tell him what was happening with Karen.

What he'd said earlier about loving her had never seemed truer than at this moment. He hurt more now than he had when she'd served him with the divorce papers. She'd made it clear that she wanted nothing to do with him, and heaven help him, he'd abide by her wishes. But no matter what the outcome of this day, it would be damn hard.

He leaned forward and clasped his hands, bracing himself against a fresh wave of pain. The hurt was so sharp, so constricting, that for a moment he found it difficult to breathe.

Distracted by his thoughts, Matt wasn't immediately aware of the doctor who entered the room and called his name.

"Matthew Caldwell."

Matt leapt to his feet and nearly tripped over a toddler sitting on the floor, stacking wooden blocks.

"I'm Matt Caldwell," he told the lanky older man in the white coat. "What's happened with Karen? What about the baby?" He prepared himself to receive the news that they hadn't been able to save the pregnancy.

"Your wife is resting comfortably."

Matt didn't bother to explain that Karen was his ex-wife.

"We've run a number of tests, and as far as we can tell the pregnancy is progressing just fine."

Matthew was too stunned to respond. "The baby's fine? What happened? Karen thought she was having a miscarriage."

The other man patted him on the back. "Your wife has a severe bladder infection."

"But...she was in such dreadful pain."

"I suspect the infection was complicated by stress and fatigue. To be on the safe side, we've decided to admit her for the night. Her obstetrician will call on her later."

"She's been dreadfully ill with morning sickness. Is this normal?"

"Sometimes. You might talk with Dr. Baker when he's in. Would you like to see your wife now?"

"Please."

Matt followed the ER physician down a corridor crowded with gurneys and IV stands to a semidarkened room. He pulled aside the thin curtain around the bed. Karen lay there, her hands resting protectively over her abdomen.

Matt barely noticed the doctor's leaving. He gazed down at Karen; their eyes met and held. She looked deathly pale against the white sheets and terribly drawn. Matt figured he probably didn't look much better. He'd never spent a more harrowing two hours in his life.

"How're you feeling?" he asked gently. Needing to touch her, Matt reached for her hand and brought it to his lips. It wasn't until her fingers closed around his that he remembered their disagreement.

"Oh, Matt," she whispered, "I'm so sorry for causing you all this trouble."

"I'd never consider helping you trouble." He kissed the back of her hand.

Tears filled her eyes and she turned her face away from him.

"The doctor said you should sleep," he urged her softly. "Don't worry about a thing."

"What about your plane? You were supposed to have left Oakland long before now." She shifted her position to look at him again.

"I called and canceled my reservation. Now stop worrying about it."

Ever so lightly, he touched her tear-stained face.

"But the tour—what about your presentations in Portland and Seattle?"

That she knew so much about his schedule surprised him. "There'll be other tours."

"I feel terrible about messing up your plans..." Her voice faded. Whatever drug the hospital had given her seemed to kick in just then, because she closed her eyes and was asleep within seconds.

Matt sat next to her bed until the orderly arrived. Then he followed Karen to the room she'd been assigned. He stayed until she started to stir, at which point he quietly slipped out. The way Matt figured it, he was the last person she'd want to see.

KAREN STARED into the emptiness, sluggish from drugs and a sleepless night spent fretting over her future and the baby's. She felt more rested now than she had in weeks. She pressed her hand against her stomach, forever grateful that the pregnancy remained intact. She'd been so afraid.

A brief smile touched her lips. Generally she was the calm, cool one in a crisis, not Matt. The reverse had happened that morning. Consumed as she was with the pain, weeping and nearly hysterical, Karen had been convinced she was suffering a miscarriage.

Although he hadn't known where to even find a hospital, Matt had been clearheaded and efficient, calling 911 for instructions and accompanying her in the ambulance. Not until they arrived at the emergency room had he displayed any emotion. And then only because the medical staff insisted he wait in the outer room.

She caught a movement out of the corner of her eye, and she turned her head to see her boss, Doug Sullivan, entering the room.

"Karen, how are you feeling?" He'd brought a large bouquet of arranged flowers and set the vase down on the nightstand.

Karen was so surprised to see him she didn't answer. "How did you know I was here?"

"Matt called me."

"Matt?" At the sound of her husband's name she swallowed hard. Apparently he'd left Oakland, because she hadn't seen him again. She'd asked the nurses about him, but no one seemed to know where he'd gone or when.

"Matt thought he should tell me you'd been hospital ized, and he was right." Doug moved to the foot of he bed. "What happened?" he asked gently.

"I don't know for sure, but all at once I had these ex cruciating pains. The doctors seem to think they're re lated to stress and fatigue."

"So Matt said."

"Was there anything else he told you?" she asked, re senting the way her ex-husband had taken it upon himsel to interfere in her life. It wouldn't bother her nearly a much if he hadn't up and disappeared without a word— which just went to prove what she'd been saying all along The man wasn't reliable.

"Matt did happen to mention that he wanted you to re turn to— What's the name of that town again?"

"Hard Luck," Karen supplied.

"Right, Hard Luck." Doug Sullivan paused, then sai in a kind voice, "It might not be such a bad idea, Karen."

"But—"

He raised his hand, stopping her. "Just until the baby' born. Matt has every right to be concerned about you . . and his baby."

The last person Karen had thought would side with he ex-husband was her boss. Typical of Matt to have some one else do his arguing for him! "Do you realize how fa Hard Luck is from Fairbanks or a town of any real size? she asked. "There isn't a doctor within a five-hundred-mil radius."

"True, but Matt says the public-health nurse is a ful qualified midwife. I believe he said her name was Dott something. She's one of the women who went up there la year—she married the shopkeeper, I think."

Karen looked away, annoyed that Matt had brought Doug in to make a case on his behalf. He was obviously very serious about getting her to move to Hard Luck.

Doug's blue eyes twinkled as he spoke. "We got quite a chuckle out of that story, remember?"

Karen wasn't likely to forget. The news article about a group of lonely bush pilots advertising for women had attracted national attention. Her own connection with Alaska had made the topic especially fascinating for everyone at the Paragon office. Karen had laughed and joked with her friends—until she'd learned that Matt had moved to Hard Luck. Then the whole story had ceased to amuse her. With women said to be arriving each and every week— a gross exaggeration, according to Lanni—Matt could easily fall in love with one of the newcomers. Why that should concern her, Karen didn't care to question.

"So this Dotty was recruited by the O'Hallorans?" Karen asked, reining in her memories.

"Yes, and then she married a guy named, let me see, Pete. Unusual last name. Lively or Liver or something."

"Livengood," Karen remembered. A man with a thick gray beard came into her mind. She'd briefly danced with him at Lanni and Charles's wedding reception.

"In addition, a doctor flies in once a month."

"You sound like you want to be rid of me," Karen complained.

"Not at all," the older man assured her, patting her hand. "You know as well as I do that I'm a mess without you. Why else do you think I personally requested you for my executive assistant when I was promoted? You deserved it as much as I did—heaven knows I wouldn't have gotten my promotion without your help."

"Nonsense." But hearing him say so helped smooth her ruffled ego.

"Come back to work next spring after the baby's born," Doug suggested. "You've been frightfully ill these last few weeks."

Karen bit down on her lip, upset at the way everyone was making decisions for her. She felt trapped and helpless. And angry.

"Nancy's doing a reasonable job of filling in for you. She's not you, but she'll do until you're back on your feet."

Karen said nothing, unwilling to agree.

"Your job will be waiting for you," Doug promised. "But right now, you need to take care of yourself and the little one."

"Did Matt put you up to this?" she asked.

"No." Once again her boss was quick to set her straight. "He came to me with a number of questions, told me what had happened and left it at that. He's worried about you, the way any husband would be."

"Matt is no longer my husband."

"I realize that, my dear, but did anyone bother to tell him? He's fiercely protective of you, Karen. I know it's bothersome, but in this instance I agree with the young man. Your health and that of the baby is what's most important."

"Yes, but—"

"Now, because I want you back, I've talked with the good people in the employment office, and if you agree, I'll arrange to have your furniture and other personal belongings placed in storage. Then later, when you're ready to return to California, everything will be here waiting for you."

The resentment she'd experienced earlier flared back to life. She didn't want anyone making that kind of decision for her. But her anger died a quick death as Karen realized Doug was acting out of genuine concern and affection. Besides, she would have come to the same conclusion herself. Her health and that of her baby's had to take priority over her distrust of her ex-husband.

Moving to Hard Luck with Matt wasn't the ideal situation, but it made more sense than any of her other options.

"What do you say, Karen?" Doug prompted.

"All right, but just until the baby's born."

"Take as long as you like," he told her, patting her hand again. "When you're ready to move back to Oakland, your job will be waiting for you."

Doug Sullivan left following their discussion, and Karen must have fallen asleep, because the next thing she knew a small noise jarred her awake. It took her a moment to realize she wasn't alone in the room.

"Sorry." Matt stood at the foot of her bed, looking sheepish. "I guess this wasn't meant to be used as a flower vase, huh?" He'd thrust a bouquet of roses into the water pitcher.

Karen couldn't keep from smiling. "You brought me flowers?"

He seemed almost embarrassed to have been caught. He shrugged and mopped up the spilled water with his handkerchief.

"Doug Sullivan was in to see me," she announced.

Matt's hand stilled as he raised his eyes to meet hers. "I suppose you're angry because I talked to him. You might as well know I phoned Dr. Baker while I was at it. You've made it plain that you don't want me meddling in your life, but there's more to consider here than—"

"I'm not angry."

His head came up as if he wasn't sure he'd heard her correctly. "You're not?"

"No. I've decided the best thing for me and the baby is to do as you suggested and move to Hard Luck with you. But I want it understood right here and now that I'm returning to California as soon as the baby's born."

Matt's expression was astonished, then ecstatic. "Whatever you say."

"Don't think you're going to change my mind, Matthew Caldwell, because it isn't going to happen."

"Whatever you say, sweetheart."

Karen groaned. "I'm not your sweetheart or anything else."

"Maybe not, but you're the mother of my baby, and for now that's all that matters."

MATT FELT LIGHTHEARTED. If he'd ever needed to prove that sometimes the quickest route to what you want is an indirect one, he'd done it with Karen. He was convinced he could have argued with her until the twelfth of never and gotten nowhere. Only when he'd received Doug Sullivan's support did he get the results he wanted.

He stared out the window of the small aircraft as it passed over the rugged Arctic terrain, heading due north toward Hard Luck. The Midnight Sons plane, piloted by Ted Richards, had picked them up in Fairbanks.

Karen slept peacefully at his side. He restrained himself from placing an arm around her, although he'd been dying to do that from the moment they'd left Oakland a day earlier.

She wasn't happy about all this, but she'd finally been willing to listen to reason. The way he figured it, once she was in his home, he'd have her back in his bed in no time, and the rest would fall naturally into place.

To begin with, he'd make sure she understood that he wasn't going to ask anything from her physically. Sexually. They'd need to sleep in the same room, though, so he'd be able to look after her properly when she was ill. That made perfect sense. Still, it might take some talking to persuade her to share a room—and a bed—with him, but he'd talk as long as he had to. Wear her down, if nothing else, he thought wryly.

Getting Karen back in his bed had haunted Matt from the night of his sister's wedding. Nothing had ever felt so right to him. That Karen should get pregnant from their one time together struck him as a kind of poetic justice.

Their lovemaking had always been incredible. That night was no exception. But it *was* an exception in another sense—they'd made love without arguing first. During the last two years of their marriage, that had become a negative pattern. They'd had a lot of fights—and always ended up in bed afterward.

No one would guess that his sweet-natured wife had such a temper. Their fights used to escalate quickly to physical comedy, with Karen throwing anything she could lay her hands on. Over the years he'd dodged books, cups, pillows. A turkey drumstick, once. And the madder she got, the more passionate she became. The hotter her temper, the hotter her desire. The fact that, with them, passion was always tied to anger disturbed him.

And it was something Karen hated about herself, this tendency to flail at her husband in anger, then reconcile in bed.

They'd broken the pattern the night of Lanni's wedding. The reality that they'd created a baby still hadn't fully sunk in. Every time he thought about it he grinned.

In the airport that very day he'd found himself watching mothers with youngsters. It was all he could do to keep from approaching total strangers and declaring that he and Karen were having a baby.

"We're almost there," he whispered. He slid his arm carefully around her; if she was going to be angry with him, then so be it.

Her beautiful long lashes fluttered open and she glanced out the small window on the opposite side of the plane. "How long have I been asleep?"

He was tempted to tell her that the amount of time she'd been awake would have been easier to calculate. "Not long," he assured her with a straight face.

She raised her eyebrows. "I'll bet. Well," she said, stretching, "I hope I can rest tonight."

She would—he'd make sure of that. Once upon a time they'd slept spoon fashion, cuddled up against each other, perfectly content. Now they would again. Every night, if he had anything to say about it.

The plane slowly descended, aligning itself with Hard Luck's narrow gravel runway. A number of planes lined the field, and several more were parked alongside nearby homes, like cars in a carport.

Matt resisted the urge to point out that the wildflowers were in bloom, to exclaim how beautiful the countryside looked with the snow all gone. June was probably his favorite month here in the high Arctic. The days were long now; night lasted only enough time for the stars to blink a couple of times and then disappear over the horizon, blinded by the light of approaching day.

"Lanni should be there to greet us," Matt assured her. When Matt had called his sister to tell her that Karen was returning with him, Lanni had shrieked with delight. She'd advised him to go slow with Karen, but he didn't need anyone to tell him that.

The Baron came down gently on the runway and coasted to a stop.

Sawyer O'Halloran was there to open the side door and lower the steps. He offered Karen his hand as she climbed out of the aircraft, then greeted her with a warm hug.

"It's *great* to see you again."

"Thanks, Sawyer," she said a bit shyly.

It gave Matt a small degree of pleasure that she didn't just blurt out that she wasn't staying once the baby was born.

Sawyer loaded the luggage into his trunk, and ten minutes later they were at the lodge. Matt was eager to see the place after his two-week absence—and eager to learn how many new reservations Lanni had taken. Thanking Sawyer, he lugged in their suitcases and set them in the lobby, then called, "Lanni!"

"She's not here," Karen informed him with perfect logic after he'd called for his sister another two times. Then he saw a note propped up on the registration desk.

"So I see," Matt said, not entirely concealing his frustration. "Well, make yourself comfortable while I put our suitcases in the bedroom." He lifted the heavy bags and headed toward the master bedroom in his private quarters—a small apartment on the main floor.

"Matt."

He set the cases back down. "Yes?"

"Where are you taking my things?"

He'd just explained that, but he was a patient man. "To the bedroom."

"You appear to be carrying them into *your* bedroom."

"Mine? It's ours now, darlin'."

Her mouth thinned in that way of hers that told him she wasn't pleased. "I believe *my* room is up the stairs—*darlin'*."

Matt's gaze followed the staircase that led to the second level and the rooms beyond. "But I thought—"

"I know exactly what you thought, Matthew Caldwell, and it's not going to happen."

In this instance, Abbey's faint might make him take
some of their talk to Duke's mind the next
time too long.

"Sawyer," she said, smiling softly. "I doesn't know why
it happened."

. . . . . .

. . . . . .

CHAPTER FIVE

ABBEY HUMMED SOFTLY to herself as she arranged the new
books on the front display table. The town council had al-
lotted her a small budget, and she'd quickly purchased the
latest hardcover releases. She didn't expect them to remain on display for very long. Now that the Hard Luck
Library was in full operation, most everyone in town took
advantage of it. Abbey had been hired to organize the library, but it was thanks to the generosity of Sawyer's
mother, Ellen O'Halloran—now Ellen Greenleaf—who
had donated a vast majority of the books, that the place
even existed. It had been Ellen's dream. And now the
people of Hard Luck had access to fiction of all kinds and
for all ages, as well as a variety of resource materials.

Abbey squatted down to replace one of the children's
books and experienced a dizzy sensation. The room started
to spin. She lost her balance and flopped onto the floor.

"Honey, I've been thinking..." Sawyer walked into the
library, halting abruptly when he found his wife sitting,
dazed, on the floor. "Abbey? Are you okay?"

She offered him a wan smile. "My goodness, that came
as a shock."

"What happened?" Sawyer asked, helping her to her
feet. He framed her face between his large hands and
studied her intently. His frown deepened. "You're pale."

"I'm a little light-headed, that's all," she said, dismiss-
ing his anxiety.

"Light-headed?" His voice turned gravelly with concern. "I think you'd better talk to Doc Gleason the next time he flies in."

"Sawyer," she said, smiling softly, "I already know why this happened."

"You do?"

"I'm about ninety-nine percent sure I'm pregnant."

"Pregnant?" Her husband's mouth fell open. "You think we're going to have a baby?" He pulled out a chair, one she thought was meant for her, then promptly sat in it himself.

Abbey laughed out loud when Sawyer placed his hand over his heart and croaked, "You might have prepared me for this."

"Sawyer, we've talked about having a baby."

"I know, but this is different... You're pregnant!"

Abbey poured him a glass of water, which he swallowed in giant gulps. "We're going to have a baby." His eyes were loving as he gazed up at her. "Oh, Abbey, I can't begin to tell you how—"

"Stunned," she said.

"No, pleased. Happy. *Thrilled..*" His lips curved in a slow smile.

She smiled back. "I know." She'd never seen her husband react quite this way to anything.

"Have you told anyone else?"

"No. Sawyer, I would tell you first. Anyway, it's still early—I'm not entirely sure myself." But she was. The joy and excitement that swelled up inside her were as unmistakable as the physical symptoms of pregnancy.

"Can I tell someone? This news is too good to keep to myself. We should let Charles and Lanni know, don't you think? My mother!" he cried. "Mom will go bananas. She's dying for a granddaughter. Just look at the way she's taken to Scott and Susan, and after three sons who can blame her for wanting a girl? We should tell Christian." He was talking so fast the words nearly blended together. "I remember the morning he started talking about bringing women to Hard Luck. I kept thinking this was the craziest idea I'd ever heard. Then I met you, and now I'm so grateful for my brother's loony ideas. Charles is grateful too—he'd never have met Lanni if we hadn't needed more housing for the—"

"Sawyer," she said, interrupting gently. She touched his arm. "Don't you think we should let Scott and Susan know before we tell anyone else?"

"Scott and Susan...of course. You mean they don't already know?"

"No, sweetheart. Of course not." He made such a comical sight it was all Abbey could do to keep from laughing.

Sawyer stood up, then immediately sat back down. "Scott can help me build the cradle. But I don't want to ignore Susan, so maybe we should—"

She placed her arms around his neck and did the only thing she could think of to silence him. She kissed him.

Slowly Sawyer eased his mouth from hers. "Abbey, we've got to—"

Determinedly she brought his mouth back to hers and kissed him again, revealing without words how much she loved him and how joyful she was to be carrying his child. This time she met with far less resistance.

Sawyer groaned and his arms circled her waist as he pulled her onto his lap. "Abbey..."

"Hmm?"

"I love you, sweetheart."

"I've never doubted that. We can tell the kids about the baby this evening, and then we'll phone your mother and let the rest of the family know."

Her kisses had mellowed him considerably. "All right, but I think you should come home and rest first."

Abbey sighed and pressed her forehead against his. "Someone needs to be at the library. Besides, we both know that if I went home neither one of us would rest."

"This is the trouble with having a wife," Sawyer muttered, grinning broadly. "You know me far too well. You're right—resting *wasn't* what I had in mind."

AS SOON AS SHE HEARD that Abbey O'Halloran was pregnant, Karen stopped by the library. She knew the building had originally been the home of Adam O'Halloran, Hard Luck's founder, and she looked around with interest.

"Karen, it's good to see you." Abbey was sitting at the large desk in the main room, working on the card catalog. "You're looking great."

"Thanks. You, too." To Karen's mixed relief and cha grin, her bouts of morning sickness had all but disap peared in the two weeks since her arrival in Hard Luck. Matt gloated, certain that her return to health could be attributed to him. Karen preferred to believe it was the fresh Alaska air.

"I understand congratulations are in order," she said to Abbey, pleased that another woman in town was preg nant, too.

"So you heard about the baby," Abbey said, smiling happily. "But then, I can't see how you *wouldn't* know. swear, Sawyer's personally announced our news to every one in Alaska. You'd think I was the only woman in the world who ever got pregnant."

"And I thought Matt was the one who believed that."

The two women chuckled. "I'm happy for you," Karen said, "and on a purely selfish note, I'm glad there's someone I can talk to about all this."

"The morning sickness is better?"

"Oh, yes," Karen said with a deep, grateful sigh. "I can't understand it. When I was in California I considered it an accomplishment if I managed to get out of bed and dress. I arrive here, and it's like a miracle cure. Oh, I still have an occasional bout of nausea, but it's nothing like what I suffered before." She didn't mention how much Matt wanted to take credit for that.

"It happens that way sometimes," Abbey told her with the wisdom of two pregnancies behind her. "Can I help you find something?" she asked. "I can recommend a couple of good books on pregnancy and infant care."

"Matt bought about a dozen books in California," Karen said with a quick grin. "Actually I came to volunteer my services."

"At the library?"

"If I could." She was eager to find something to occupy her time. Matt was busy with the lodge, and she rarely saw him more than twenty minutes a day. Although she was living with her ex-husband, Karen was lonelier than before. The first set of guests had arrived, and Matt had left for a two-day fishing expedition; he wouldn't return until sometime that afternoon. But before leaving he'd hired Diane Hestead, a high school girl, as a part-time maid.

"I'd like to volunteer my services for the wedding reception for Mitch and Bethany Harris, too." Lanni had told Karen that the couple had been married ten days earlier in San Francisco. A huge welcoming party was planned for them when they returned from their honeymoon.

"We'd love to have you if you're sure you feel up to it," Abbey said excitedly.

Karen was tired of sitting around the lodge with nothing to do—no defined tasks. No responsibilities. Twiddling her thumbs. She'd even taken to organizing Matt's office, although she wasn't sure how he'd feel about it. He might have studied accounting, but the man didn't know the meaning of the words "filing system." Earlier that morning, Karen had gone into his office to set the mail on his desk and couldn't find a bare space.

How he could manage anything in such clutter was beyond her. She'd left the mail, determined to remind her ex husband that this was no way to run a business. Ten minutes later she'd returned to the office and tackled the mess herself. Before she realized it, the morning was gone and she'd set up a filing system for him.

Although she told herself she'd done it out of her own need for organization, she knew that wasn't entirely true. She wanted to help Matt. Contribute.

He hadn't asked one thing of her. He treated her like a guest, and that wasn't what she wanted. If she was going to make the lodge her home for the next five or six months, then it was important to do something in return. She wanted to be part of the community, too, and helping with this reception was a good start.

Abbey beamed. "Ben insisted on doing all the cooking. Mariah Douglas—she's the Midnight Sons secretary, in case you haven't met her—is working on the decorations. Dotty Livengood's helping, too."

Karen was eager to make friends with the other women in Hard Luck. She hadn't ventured far from the lodge and was still finding her way around the small community. Everyone seemed to know her, though, thanks to Matt.

"The reception's on Saturday," Abbey continued, "and from what I understand, Mariah and Dotty are hoping to get everyone together Friday evening around seven to decorate. We'd love it if you'd come."

"I'll be there," Karen promised.

The July sun shone brightly as she wandered slowly back to the lodge, enjoying the day's warmth and the friendly greetings. Matt hadn't given her a specific time to expect him home, but she hoped it would be soon.

The first thing Karen noticed when she stepped into the lodge was the inviting smells coming from the kitchen. Savory spices mingled with the scent of simmering beef and vegetables.

"Matt?" She found her husband in the kitchen, wearing a starched white apron. He stood in front of the stove and grinned wryly when he saw her.

"Hi, honey, I'm home."

Karen begrudged the way her heart leapt with excitement just to see him again. She was lonely, she told herself, that was all. What did she expect when family and friends were in Anchorage, hundreds of miles away?

"How'd everything go?" she asked in an effort to take her mind off her pleasure at having him home.

"Great. The guys are showering up now. We had a fabulous time."

"Did you catch any fish?" Matt wasn't likely to get much repeat business unless he supplied the fishing experience of a lifetime. Karen had read in one of those glossy travel publications that it was cheaper to go on a safari in Africa than an expedition in Alaska.

"Both men said this was the best fishing of their lives. They've already given me a deposit for next year."

Karen couldn't help sharing in his pride. "That's wonderful!"

Matt added chopped potato to the stew. "Did you mis
me?"

She had, but she wasn't about to admit it. "You wer
only gone two days."

"That doesn't answer my question."

She knew what he was hoping to hear; she just didn'
think it was a good idea to let him know how lonely she'
been. "It was quiet around here," she said unwillingly.

He couldn't seem to take his eyes off her. "I swea
you're looking more beautiful every day. Pregnancy ob
viously becomes you."

Compliments generally made Karen uncomfortable. "
can't button my jeans. And I'm only three months along,
she complained. "At this rate, I'll end up resembling
battleship."

He stepped away from the stove and made a show c
studying her. He twisted his head one way and then th
other. When he'd finished, he said in a thoughtful ton
"Maybe, but you'll be the prettiest battleship around."

Matt always knew how to cheer her up. But she didn
want to laugh and joke with him; that kind of camar
derie was dangerous. She had to remind herself repea
edly that after the baby was born, she was returning t
California. It was becoming more and more difficult t
think about her life away from Matt.

"Let me help you with dinner," she insisted.

"No way." He was prepared to chase her out of th
kitchen, but she stood her ground.

"Matt, I want to help. If you don't let me I'll go craz
with nothing to do."

He gave in. "All right, all right. You can set the table.

Then, because she was pleased to see him, and becaus
she forgot for a moment that they were divorced and li

ing together as brother and sister, she stood on her tiptoes and briefly brushed his mouth with hers.

Matt stared at her as though she'd suddenly sprouted wings. Or antennae. His expression said he didn't understand why she'd done this. She wasn't sure herself. But it felt right. It felt more than right—it felt *good*.

THE FOLKS IN HARD LUCK were getting to be experts at celebrating weddings, Ben Hamilton mused contentedly. He worked in the compact kitchen beside the school gymnasium, assembling hors d'oeuvres for Bethany and Mitch. First there'd been a wedding and reception for Sawyer and Abbey, and almost directly afterward another for Pete and Dotty. Come spring there was Charles and Lanni's, and now a reception for Bethany and Mitch.

His gaze followed the couple as they circulated among their guests. A swell of pride filled him as he regarded Bethany—his daughter. The realization still took some getting used to. He actually had a daughter. One he'd never known about until she'd arrived in Hard Luck last year.

It saddened Ben to acknowledge that he hadn't been there for either Bethany or her mother, Marilyn. Instead, he'd spent twenty-odd years in the United States Navy, first in Vietnam and later on various ports around the world. When he retired ten years ago, only in his forties, he'd come here to Alaska and opened his café. He'd never married; his affair with Marilyn was a brief episode he'd never forgotten. One that, it turned out, had left him with a daughter.

And my, oh my, Bethany was a pretty thing. Looking at her now with her husband and stepdaughter, Chrissie, Ben wondered how he could have produced such a charming, caring woman.

With more than a touch of regret, he realized he hadn't. Her mother and Peter Ross, the man who'd loved Marilyn, had raised Bethany; they were the ones responsible for the woman she'd become. His contribution to the effort had been strictly genetic. Still, he took a good deal of pleasure in the woman she'd become. It thrilled him no end that Bethany and Mitch had decided to continue living in Hard Luck. He hadn't defined what role he would play in her life yet, but he was grateful for the opportunity to know her.

"What are you doing in the kitchen?" Christian O'Halloran demanded. "You should be out there with everyone else, enjoying the party."

Ben wasn't comfortable outside of a kitchen. He found he related to folks far more easily when he had something to occupy his hands, when he had coffee to pour and food to serve. He never had been one to mix and mingle at parties.

"I've got plenty to do right here," he insisted. He had the hors d'oeuvre platters ready, plus the fruit and vegetable trays. Fine-looking trays, too, even if he said so himself.

He'd spent a lot of time making sure everything was as appealing to the eye as it was to the palate. That he'd borrowed a cookbook by Martha Stewart from the library was his and Abbey's secret.

"But this is Bethany and Mitch's reception," Christian told him, as if he didn't already know.

"Ben, what can I do to help?" Mariah Douglas stepped into the kitchen and stopped abruptly when she saw Christian O'Halloran. The two regarded each other like wary dogs.

Ben had never considered himself much of an expert when it came to dealing with women. He was a crusty old bachelor, set in his ways. Nevertheless, he liked to think he was a good judge of what was happening between people. It seemed to him that Mariah Douglas was sweet on Christian—which was unfortunate, because the youngest O'Halloran brother avoided Mariah like a communicable disease.

"Hello, Christian," she greeted him stiffly.

Considering they worked together every day, it amazed Ben that Mariah was actually blushing.

"Mariah." Christian nodded once, formally, and Ben noticed that he backed up several steps.

Mariah returned her attention to Ben. "Can I help?"

"I've already offered," Christian said.

If Christian hoped those curt words would dismiss her, his plan failed. Ben decided it was time to intervene. "These trays could do with replacing, and that punch bowl needs to be refilled and set out on the table," he said briskly. Someone had brought the almost empty bowl into the kitchen. "Must be plenty of thirsty folks."

Ignoring Christian, Mariah headed for the punch bowl.

Christian started to lift a tray, then hesitated when he saw Mariah. "Don't do it like that."

"Like what?" she snapped.

Ben didn't blame her for using that tone. He wasn't privy to what was going on between them, but he'd listened to Christian's complaints about his inept secretary often enough to feel some sympathy for her.

"Don't fill the punch bowl here," Christian muttered as if that should have been obvious. "Did you stop to think how much easier it would be to carry the bowl to the table first and *then* mix the punch?" He gestured to the wine, soda water and fruit juice lined up on the counter.

"Yes, but—"

"Here, I'll do that and you carry the trays out."

"No," Mariah insisted. "I said I'd take care of this. Stop worrying about me."

Christian and Mariah reached for the punch bowl at the same time. Ben could see it coming even before it happened. As they tugged at opposite sides of the bowl, the bright red remains of the punch swirled around the bottom and upward in a wave—which slapped Christian's white dress shirt and ran down the front of his pants. He gasped and leapt back.

"Christian!" Mariah cried with alarm. "Oh, no."

"Now look what you've done!" Christian shouted.

"Me? As far as I'm concerned, you brought this on yourself."

Ben was proud to see that Mariah had learned to hold her own against her employer. She didn't even blink as he glared at her.

Christian's eyes narrowed and he whirled around to leave the kitchen. "Tell Mitch and Bethany I'll be back as soon as I've changed clothes," he said to Ben.

The instant Christian was out the door, Mariah sagged against the counter.

"You all right?" Ben asked.

"I'm fine," she muttered. "It's just that Christian and I... Oh, never mind. I'm sorry, Ben."

"No need to apologize to me." He picked up the food tray himself and carried it out to the table, then stepped back to admire his work. He grinned, inordinately pleased with his effort. It was a small thing, but he felt pride in being able to contribute to his daughter's reception.

"Ben." Bethany joined him. "I don't know how Mitch and I can possibly thank you. Everything looks so beautiful."

Ben decided he could live on those words and the happiness gleaming in her eyes for at least a week. "It's nothing," he said with a nonchalant shrug, as if he'd whipped up the entire display that morning. In actuality, he'd been planning and working on it for weeks.

"The food's fabulous," Bethany told him, "And I know what those grapes and watermelons cost. You've done such a beautiful job." She stood on tiptoe to kiss his cheek.

"I wanted your party to be special," he said, uneasy with emotion, even positive emotion. Damn, but he was proud of Bethany.

She'd chosen a good man in Mitch, too. Ben grinned. He was pretty gauche about this romance business, but he was well aware that Mitch's daughter was responsible for bringing her father and Bethany—her teacher—together. It amazed him that an eight-year-old girl could be so smart. Ben was convinced he couldn't have picked a better man for Bethany had he sought out a husband for her himself.

"Dad told me what you did," Bethany said, slipping her arm around Ben's waist. "Writing Mom and Dad that letter was really thoughtful."

He shrugged again, making light of the single most difficult letter he'd ever written. "It was nothing."

"Dad told me you thanked him for raising me so well. It wasn't easy telling my folks I'd found you, and I think Dad might have harbored some fear that you'd replace him in my life."

Ben had given that some consideration, too. Peter Ross deserved a lot of credit for marrying a young woman pregnant with another man's child, and raising that baby to be the beautiful, generous woman Bethany had become. Ben wanted to thank this man he'd never met, and at the same time reassure him that he had no intention of stealing his daughter away. Peter was her real father; he respected that. Ben felt it was time to clear the slate with Marilyn, too. He'd written his regrets to Bethany's mother and asked her to forgive him for having left her to deal with the pregnancy alone.

"Dad said he'd be pleased to count you as a friend," Bethany told him, eyes glistening with tears.

Ben already knew that. Peter's letter had arrived two days before Bethany's wedding, and Marilyn had written him, also. He'd loved her, Ben realized; perhaps he still did. But he was content; she was happy and he'd discovered a woman who was not only his daughter but his comfort, his friend. Everything had worked out for the best.

"Are you going to dance with me?" Bethany asked, hugging him.

"Dance? Me?" Ben experienced a fleeting moment of panic. "Not on your life. That's what you've got a husband for. Now let me get back to the kitchen before your guests get hungry." He hurried back to where he felt most at home, but he turned around to study his daughter one last time. His heart seemed to expand a bit as Bethany stepped onto the dance floor with Mitch.

MATT KNEW Karen was having a good time. He'd been counting on this wedding reception for Bethany and Mitch. The last time the people of Hard Luck had gathered to celebrate a wedding was the night Karen had spent with him. Matt sincerely hoped that history was about to repeat itself.

He'd certainly been restraining himself with his ex-wife—he'd been as good as a choirboy! In three weeks he'd hadn't even *tried* to kiss her, which was a real feat, considering how he felt about her.

Matt feared she was looking for an excuse to leave, something that would prove she'd be better off living elsewhere. True, her options were limited right now; nevertheless she did have some. For example, he knew that her parents had invited her to move home if things became too uncomfortable. But Matt had decided he wasn't going to give Karen any reason to leave Hard Luck. He had five and a half months to prove himself. Five and a half very short months.

His hands-off policy was working, too; Matt could tell. She was much more relaxed with him. And almost against her will, she was beginning to appreciate the simple life in Hard Luck. She'd become part of the community, made new friends. And having his sister in town had proved more of an advantage than he'd anticipated. The two women got together at least twice a week.

Because she wanted to keep busy, Karen had started volunteering two afternoons a week at the library. In a matter of days she was more familiar with the townsfolk than he was after living in Hard Luck for nearly a year.

Another thing that boded well was the interest she'd taken in the lodge itself. Without his saying a word, Karen had started adding those small feminine touches he'd hoped for.

Before he knew it, she'd draped a patchwork quilt over the back of the sofa. A vase of wildflowers magically appeared at the registration desk. She'd even brought in a number of pieces of scrimshaw and some jade figurines. One day, out of the blue, a hand-carved totem pole appeared over the fireplace; it looked perfect, as though it had always stood there. She never said where she got it or how much she'd paid. Now and again, he found her looking at it and smiling happily to herself.

Over dinner a couple of nights before, she'd offered him a suggestion—a damn good one too. She'd pointed out that the lodge was attracting tourists from all over North

America, and in order to reach Hard Luck they had to fly over the Arctic Circle. Karen came up with the idea of having certificates printed for everyone who stayed at the lodge, making them official members of the Arctic Circle Club. The next thing he knew, she was flipping through catalogs and making more suggestions. Like selling coffee mugs with the lodge's name and logo. That was a good idea, he agreed, especially if people took them home and used them at the office. Nothing like free advertising.

He was encouraged by all these indications of her growing attachment to Hard Luck and the lodge. But the most promising sign so far was the difference in her attitude toward him. Even if their relationship was more comradely than romantic. Or possibly because of that.

Okay, so he'd been out of line thinking they should sleep together right away. It was an innocent mistake. They weren't exactly strangers; besides, she was pregnant with his child. He'd assumed . . . and he shouldn't have. It was taking far longer than he'd expected for her sensibilities to right themselves.

Damn it all, Matt wanted her with him. His bed had never seemed so big . . . and empty. Every night he lay on his back and stared at the ceiling, knowing the woman he loved, the woman pregnant with his child, slept in the room directly above him. If ever there was a guarantee of insomnia, Karen had provided it.

On a more positive note everything else in his life seemed to be falling satisfactorily into place. With reservations coming in for the dogsledding tours and the business he'd managed to pick up this summer, there was a good possibility he'd break even. Well, perhaps not this year, but the next for sure. At the moment he was content to meet his expenses. The lodge was an investment, and for the first time since he'd told Karen about it, she was beginning to see the promise.

He watched her now, laughing with her friends, hugging Bethany, wishing the young couple well, and Matt grew impatient. Dancing had started an hour ago, and he wanted her in his arms.

Joining Karen, he slipped an arm around her waist. If he hadn't known she was pregnant, it would have been hard to tell. But he did know, and he found himself conscious of the thickening about her middle. Matt was convinced that this baby was giving him a second chance with Karen.

"How about a dance?" he asked. He'd had a couple of beers with the guys and was feeling mellow. Mellow enough to put aside his inhibitions.

"A dance?" She gazed up at him, frowning slightly as if she wasn't sure they should.

"One dance," he pleaded softly. They were halfway onto the dance floor already; she could hardly refuse.

"One dance," she echoed.

God was on his side, Matt decided, because the song was a lovely old ballad from the sixties, the music slow and sultry. Matt drew Karen into the circle of his arms, maintaining a respectable distance between them. Just enough to reassure her.

To his delight she leaned closer and pressed her head against his shoulder. "I love weddings," she murmured.

Matt was beginning to share her feelings. She hummed along with the music, and he closed his eyes, remembering the days when she came to him without restraint, without reserve. Remembering the times she'd freely shared her love.

One dance quickly became two, and then three. It felt so
familiar—as if she'd never left him, never stopped loving
him, never gone through with the divorce.

When Matt looked up, he noticed that a good number
of the townsfolk had already left. By tacit agreement, he
led Karen outside; together they strolled back to the lodge.

Once home it seemed only natural to kiss her. It was
what he'd longed to do for weeks, what had been on his
mind for days, ever since he'd learned they'd be attending
the reception.

Karen sighed when his lips met hers. She tasted of summer and sunshine, tasted of heaven. Knowing this was
what they both wanted, Matt deepened the kiss. His heart
nearly flew out of his chest at the way her arms tightened
around him. He caressed her back, savoring her softness.
He investigated the slender curve of her spine and sought
the curved fullness of her hips. He pulled her closer,
needing her, wanting her to know exactly how much.

"Karen, I love you. I'm so damned crazy about you,"
he whispered between kisses.

"Oh, Matt..."

He kissed her again with a sweet desperation. "You
know what I want," he murmured huskily when the kiss
ended.

Karen braced her forehead against his shoulder and drew
in several deep breaths. "I...I think it's time I went upstairs."

"Upstairs? You mean you aren't—you won't—" He
stopped abruptly. He opened his mouth to argue with her,
then closed it, knowing it would do no good.

"Good night, Matt," she said, and kissed his cheek.
"Thank you for a lovely, romantic evening." With that
she turned and walked up the stairs. Alone.

CHAPTER SIX

KAREN HAD BEEN more tempted to sleep with Matt than she ever wanted him to know. It shocked her how easily he could take her in. How susceptible she was. She'd been in Hard Luck less than a month, and already he'd half persuaded her to accept his dream, the same way he had so many times before.

Already he had her believing in the lodge, in the feasibility of its success. Only, Karen should have known better—*did* know better. She'd walked that path too often not to recognize what awaited her at the end.

This latest scheme would be like all the others. Matt would completely win her over and then, when she least expected it, he'd abandon the entire venture for some ridiculous reason. Their past was riddled with such incidents. Her father had repeatedly done the same thing to her mother. It still astonished Karen that out of all the men in the universe, she had to marry one just like him. Yet, Karen reminded herself, she dearly loved her father. He had his faults, true, and they were glaring, but like Matt, he was a good man.

She could feel herself weakening. She loved living in Hard Luck and had quickly formed friendships. The sense of community and family was strong, and that appealed to her, especially now. People cared about each other. And like all of Alaska, the scenery was spectacular.

From her bedroom window she had a stunning view of the Brooks Mountains. She could see blooming tundra, awash with colorful wildflowers. The beauty of the landscape was almost more than any one person could absorb.

It went without saying that in January, when the baby was due, the world outside her window would be a different one. In the dead of winter, daylight would be minimal. Temperatures would dip to thirty and forty below. She'd lived in Alaska a long time, though, and that didn't really alarm her.

Karen stood gazing out her window at the morning and mulled over the situation with Matt. What was it about weddings and slow dancing that made her weaken her resolve every time?

A bright red warning light had started flashing in her mind the moment Matt led her onto the dance floor. She'd known even before he kissed her what was likely to happen. Yet, wanting him the way she did, she'd been powerless to stop.

If she didn't develop some control over her strong sexual attraction to him, it could quickly become a problem.

The obvious solution was to accept her parents' offer to move to Anchorage with them until the baby was born. The thought depressed her so much she immediately dismissed it. She closed her eyes, remembering all the places she'd lived as a child. They'd moved so often, never planted roots in any one town. Karen refused to live that migratory existence ever again. And she didn't want to be reminded of all those distressing emotions, all those sad childhood times—especially when she was about to have a child of her own.

It took some doing to own up to the truth: she didn't want to leave Hard Luck. Nor did she want to be separated from Matt, not now, not while she was pregnant.

Later, she told herself, after the baby was born she'd visit her parents before she headed back to California.

She dressed and wandered downstairs. Yawning, she stretched her arms high above her head, surprised by how good she felt.

Matt, who stood behind the reservation desk, glanced up at her. "You look well rested," he murmured dryly.

"I am." Briefly she wondered what had happened to his usual cheerful greeting. She'd heard a joke long ago that said there were two kinds of people in the world—those who woke up in the morning and said, "Good morning, God," and those who said, "Good God, morning!" Karen had her own observation to add; she'd noticed that these two very different types of people often found one another—and married.

Matt fell into the chipper, lighthearted category and she into the other. Mornings had never been her favorite time of day, although it was easier when she had a regular schedule. This basic difference between them went further than simply the way they reacted to mornings. Matt was an optimist; she, however, was a realist. Or so she'd always insisted.

This particular morning she felt good—for no particular reason. Humming softly to herself, she poured a glass of orange juice and carried it to the front desk. "I'm meeting Lanni today," she said, sipping the juice.

Matt gave her a perfunctory nod of acknowledgment, then returned his attention to the ledger.

"Is something bothering you?" she asked.

"Not a damn thing," he snapped.

"My, my, we're in a grumpy mood this morning."

He glared at her.

Then it hit Karen like a ton of glacial ice. Her ex-husband was actually sulking because she'd refused to go to bed with him. This wasn't like Matt, either. As long as she'd known him, he'd never been subject to mood swings. Rarely, if ever, was Matt in a bad mood.

Some of the difficulties in their marriage had come from his almost childish insistence that everything would work out. Everything would be fine. He refused to look at any problem seriously, or even acknowledge there *was* a problem. This moody self-absorption was a side of him she hadn't seen, and frankly it amused her. She smiled.

"What's so funny?" he demanded.

"You. Matthew Caldwell, you're pouting."

"I most certainly am not." He slammed the ledger closed. "If there's anything wrong with me—and rest assured there isn't—it's that I didn't sleep well last night."

Karen didn't ask why; she knew. Their pattern had been broken. The fighting, followed by the intense lovemaking. They'd made progress, whether Matt recognized it or not.

He released a long sigh and shook his head. With a quick wave Karen started out the door, eager to see Lanni.

"Karen." Matt stopped her. "You said something last night that intrigued me."

"I did?"

"Before you went upstairs, you thanked me for the romantic evening."

"Yes?" she asked, not understanding his question.

"What made last night romantic?"

She shrugged. "I don't know. The way we danced, I guess. The way you held me, the way we kissed..."

"But you didn't spend the night with me."

This was another area of dissension that had often annoyed Karen. "Don't confuse sex with romance. A woman likes to be...wooed." She shrugged. "It's an old-fashioned word, I know, but it's what I mean."

"Wooed." Matt repeated the word as if it contained magic. His eyes brightened.

"I suspect it's not a good idea to tell you this, but you tempted me last night," Karen said. "It was all I could do to refuse you."

A cocky grin spread across his face. "Really." Almost immediately he started to frown. "If that's the case, why didn't you? You've got to know how much I love you, how much I want us to get back together again."

She stared down at the floor, not ready to admit that she wanted it, too. "I need more time," she said, knowing that sounded lame. But it was the truth.

"What if I wooed you just like you said?" he suggested. "Would that help?"

She looked at Matt and trembled with dread. Because, without a doubt, it was already too late. She loved him, loved the lodge, loved living in Hard Luck.

"Karen?" he asked again.

"I think it might be a good thing for us both," she answered. And then, afraid of what the future held, she hurried out the door.

MATT GLEEFULLY TOSSED his ballpoint pen into the air and caught it. He didn't know why he hadn't thought of this sooner. The solution was so simple! All this time, and he'd overlooked the obvious.

Every woman wanted to be shown that she was loved and appreciated. He needed to prove this to Karen, and he needed to do it clearly and conclusively. He had to give her a reason to marry him again—other than the obvious one that she was pregnant with his child. He'd assumed that should be enough, but if he'd learned anything in his four-year marriage it was that women were rarely practical when it came to matters of the heart.

With the same determination he'd brought to rebuilding the lodge, he decided to take on the project of wooing back his ex-wife.

Soon, however, his grin faded. He set the pen down on the registration desk and wiped a hand across his suddenly damp brow.

Karen wanted to be wooed. How the hell was he supposed to do that?

"WHAT DO YOU THINK?" Lanni asked, studying Karen as her friend turned to the last page. This was agony, and Lanni chewed her lower lip, anticipating Karen's reaction to her latest article.

Charles had read the piece and raved about it, but Charles was her husband and, crazy as she was about him, she doubted he was a good judge of her work. According to him, she was simply brilliant. Although she loved him for believing that, she needed a less biased opinion.

Karen, on the other hand, could have been an editor.

Her former sister-in-law sighed and straightened the stack of pages.

"Well?" Lanni asked, barely giving Karen time to breathe. She yanked out the chair and sat across the table from her. "Tell me what you think. You don't need to worry about upsetting me. I just want the truth."

"The truth," Karen repeated. "Lanni, this is a beautifully written piece."

Lanni loved hearing it. "You think so? You really think so?"

"Have you decided where you want to submit it?"

Lanni named a nationwide, glossy travel periodical and waited for Karen to suggest she aim for a regional magazine, instead.

"Sounds like a good idea."

"You think so?" Her vocabulary seemed to be limited to those three words.

"Lanni, you should have more confidence in your talent. This article about Mt. McKinley is one of the best-written and best-researched I've ever read. This past year..." She hesitated. "I'm not sure how to put it, but there's a maturity to your writing that was lacking earlier. I'm sure the apprenticeship program with the Anchorage newspaper helped, but you've acquired more than style or technical skill."

Lanni hung on every word.

"Your work shows a new...depth."

Loving Charles had done that for her; Lanni was convinced of it. Their love, their marriage, had changed her view of life, deepened her understanding of people, given her a greater sympathy and tolerance. Charles had also helped her develop a more profound appreciation for the land.

They'd waited eight months, until she was finished the apprenticeship program, before they'd married. If it had been her decision she would have married Charles last Christmas, but he'd been the one to insist they hold off until she'd fulfilled her obligation to the paper. He'd worried about the fact that he was ten years older, and it was almost as if he expected her to change her mind. But not once had she doubted that she was meant to be with Charles O'Halloran. Nor did she doubt his love.

For years their two families had hated each other. Catherine Fletcher, Lanni's grandmother, had brought nothing but pain into the O'Hallorans' lives. David O'Halloran, Charles's father, was the only man her grandmother had ever loved. Yet Catherine had done all she could to hurt him, because he'd hurt her. Wrongs had been committed on both sides.

David and Catherine were both dead now. Lanni was sure they'd approve of her marriage and the reconciliation it had brought. Despite the animosity between their families, she and Charles had fallen in love. In some ways, she believed they were soul mates, meant for each other. It sounded fanciful, but she'd come to think they'd been given this one opportunity to make up for the wrongs of the past.

"There're a couple of typos," Karen murmured, flipping through the pages. She pointed them out, then swallowed the last of her cold drink. "I wish I could put my finger on what's changed in your writing."

Lanni smiled to herself. She didn't need Karen to tell her. She already knew.

MATT SLID onto a stool in the Hard Luck Café. Anyone who needed advice sought out Ben Hamilton. Although he'd never been married most people thought of him as something of an expert when it came to relationships.

"Coffee?" Ben asked, gesturing with the pot.

"No, thanks. I came in for a little advice." Matt wanted to get straight to the point.

"You're not going to order anything?"

"No, I wanted to ask—"

"Listen, advice is no longer free," Ben said. "You sit back and chow down on a piece of my homemade applepie, and then I'll tell you whatever it is you want to know."

"I'm not hungry," Matt objected. He'd never known Ben to push food on anyone. "Business slow or something?"

"All these women in town aren't exactly helping, you know? Every one of them's got a kitchen, and if they haven't already got a family to cook for, they're inviting the men in town to dinner. Business is down twenty percent from a year ago.''

It looked like Matt was going to be the one with the sympathetic ear.

"So that's what the frequent-eater program's all about?"

"Exactly."

Matt understood Ben's concern, and he did want to support the Hard Luck Café. "All right, give me a cup of coffee." He was desperate enough to pay for coffee he didn't want if Ben could help him win over Karen.

Ben nodded, obviously pleased. He filled Matt's cup, then pressed his hands against the counter. "What can I do for you?"

"It's about Karen."

Ben's mouth quivered with the telltale signs of a smile. "Goes without saying."

Once more Matt was as direct as possible. "She wants to be, uh, *wooed.*"

"Wooed," Ben repeated as though he'd never heard the word before. "What exactly does that mean?"

Matt hadn't considered that Ben wouldn't know. It would be a damn shame to waste a couple of bucks on a cup of brew if Ben wasn't going to help him. "Why the hell do you think I'm asking you?"

The door opened and Sawyer O'Halloran walked in.

"Sawyer," Ben called out, looking relieved. "You got a minute?"

"Sure." Sawyer perched on the stool next to Matt's.

"Matt, here, has a problem. Maybe you could help."

"Be glad to do anything I can," he said, righting his mug.

"Karen wants to be wooed," Matt told him.

"Any ideas?" Ben asked the pilot.

Sawyer frowned as he took his first sip of coffee. "You're asking the wrong fellow. I know what the word means, in a general way, but how to go about it is another question."

"You convinced Abbey to marry you," Ben reminded him.

"Sure, but it wasn't easy."

"How'd you do it?" Matt asked. True, he'd been married himself, married to Karen, but they were both young then. He didn't remember that he'd done anything special. She'd apparently thought marriage was a good idea, and he'd gone along with it. God knew he loved her. There hadn't been any talk of this wooing business; it sure hadn't been the problem it was now.

"First I didn't realize I was in love with Abbey," Sawyer confessed. "All I knew was I didn't like any of the other men bugging her. When I heard Pete Livengood had proposed I went ballistic."

"Pete's married to Dotty," Matt said, confused.

"That was before Dotty arrived," Ben explained.

"Okay, so Pete proposed to Abbey."

"It made me damn mad," Sawyer muttered. "I told myself that Christian and I had brought these women up to Hard Luck and it had cost us a lot of money. I sure as hell hadn't gone through all that trouble and expense so the local grocer, twenty years Abbey's senior, could steal her away."

"So what'd you do?" Matt asked.

"I did the only logical thing I could think of. I told her if she was that desperate to find a husband, I'd marry her myself."

Wow, maybe this'll be easier than I assumed, Matt thought. "Great idea. And that worked?"

Ben chuckled. "It worked so good the next thing I heard, Abbey had packed her bags and was scheduled to leave on the first flight out of here."

"You're joking." Matt could see they weren't. "So what'd you do next?"

Sawyer held his mug with both hands and frowned. "What could I do? I begged."

"Begged?" Matt figured he'd already tried that and it hadn't worked.

"I'd never been lower in my life. If there'd been any bridges around here, I might have jumped," Sawyer said, chuckling. "One thing I knew for sure—if Abbey left I wouldn't be worth a damn. I loved her and Scott and Susan."

"What did you say that convinced her?"

Sawyer mulled that over, then shook his head. "Hell if I know. I was just so grateful she agreed to marry me I never asked."

The door opened again and ten-year-old Scott O'Halloran flew into the café.

"Don't be bringing that dog in here," Ben warned.

Scott said something to Eagle Catcher, who stopped abruptly, tail drooping between his legs, and turned around. With a backward glance he ambled out the door.

"I swear that husky understands English," Matt said.

"I'll only be a minute," Scott told the dog. He hurried to the counter and slapped down a dollar bill. "Have you got any of those ice-cream bars left, Ben?"

"Sure do." Ben turned and headed for the freezer in the kitchen.

"So Karen wants to be wooed," Sawyer said to Matt. "She wants to be courted."

Wooed. Courted. Whatever you called it, Matt still didn't have any clearer idea of what she was seeking than before he'd asked his friends. He knew the results he was after; he understood the general strategy, but he just didn't have any specific plans.

"That's a good idea," Scott murmured absently.

"What is?" Matt asked the boy.

"Courting Karen. I wish she would marry you again, because then Angie or Davey would have someone to play with after they're born."

"Those are the names Abbey, the kids and I've got picked out for the baby," Sawyer explained. "You might listen to Scott—he offered me some valuable advice when I needed it with Abbey.

"Really?" Matt said eagerly. He didn't believe a ten-year-old kid could supply him with the answer three adult men couldn't. "So you think it's a good idea for me to court my ex-wife?"

Ben returned with the ice-cream bar. Scott regarded the others suspiciously. "Yeah," he said as if he thought this might be a trick question.

"Got any ideas how a man's supposed to go about that?" Ben asked Scott, leaning halfway over the counter.

"Well," Scott said, clearing his throat, "he could flatter her."

The three men exchanged glances. "That sounds like a good idea," Ben said.

"Yeah. Tell her . . . tell her that her eyes are as brown as a bear's winter coat," Sawyer suggested.

"She's got blue eyes," Matt said.

"Blue . . . blue . . ." Sawyer repeated in an apparent effort to find something to compare to her blue eyes. He must have said the word ten times before he stopped, defeated. "Anyone else got any ideas? I'm not exactly a poet, you know."

Matt had already figured that out for himself.

"Be affectionate," Scott suggested next.

The three leapt on that like hungry wolves over fresh kill. Matt was the first one to realize it wouldn't work.

"But . . . Karen's already pregnant," he babbled. Good grief, he can't get any more affectionate than that.

"True," Sawyer agreed.

"What about flowers?" Ben threw out. "Women are supposed to be crazy about getting flowers."

Matt had already thought of that himself. First he didn't have the money for such extravagance. And second, "Why would she want flowers when the tundra's in full bloom?"

"Maybe you should pick her some," Ben said.

Matt dismissed the idea with a sharp shake of his head. "I've got better things to do than traipse around there looking for tulips."

"There aren't any tulips on the tundra," Sawyer told him.

"I know that!" Matt snapped, losing patience. He glanced at Scott again. "Got any other ideas?"

The kid was busy eating his ice-cream bar, and Matt could tell from the way Scott kept looking over his shoulder that he was eager to be back outside with his dog. "Romance her," he said tersely.

"Romance," Matt echoed. That was what he'd thought this entire conversation had been about in the first place.

"Can I go now?" Scott asked him.

"You can go." Matt removed the dollar bill from the counter and handed it back to the boy. "Put that on my tab, Ben," he instructed. "Thanks for your help, Scott."

The boy was gone in a flash.

"Just a minute!" Sawyer leapt off his stool. "Man, why didn't I think of this sooner? I've got the perfect solution for you."

Matt was paying attention now. "You do?"

"Hot damn, I can't believe I didn't think of this sooner." Sawyer paced the floor, threading his way between the tables. He slapped his hand against his thigh. "One of the most romantic things Abbey and I ever did was fly out to Abbey Lake."

"Abbey Lake."

"Yeah, I named it after her. She got a real kick out of that."

"I don't own any lakes to name after Karen." Matt was losing confidence again. Unlike him, the O'Hallorans owned a lot of land in these parts and could easily afford to name lakes after the women in their lives. Besides, land wasn't available to the everyday citizen the way it used to be, before statehood.

Sawyer gave an exasperated sigh. "I'm not saying you should name a lake after Karen. I'm saying you should take her into the wilderness with you."

"Fishing?"

"Why not?" Sawyer asked.

"Yeah," Ben echoed, "why not?"

Matt couldn't think of a reason not to do it. "You seriously think she'd like that?"

"Abbey thought it was great fun. I flew her and the kids out to the lake. Must have been a little more than a year ago now," Sawyer continued. "It was one of those really hot summer days we get now and then."

"Had quite a hot spell last year about this time," Ben commented. "That was when I served sweet-and-sour meatballs with pineapple for dinner one night. Sort of my salute-to-the-tropics night. John Henderson ate two platefuls." Ben grinned proudly. "I had those little umbrellas sticking out of the meatballs. They looked real festive."

"Go on," Matt encouraged Sawyer, afraid that Ben might have distracted him.

"I remember it was one of the first times I ever kissed Abbey. The kids were there having a great time in the water." His eyes grew warm with the memory. "That was when I realized how much I liked being with her."

"You must have if you were kissing her," Ben muttered. He reached for the coffee and topped up their mugs.

Still, Matt was skeptical. "I'm not so sure if Karen's the outdoor type."

"You think Abbey is?" Sawyer asked.

Sawyer had a point. The idea started to build in Matt's mind. The two of them out in the Alaskan tundra. Alone . . . It led to all kinds of interesting possibilities.

"Tell her if she's going to be answering the phone at the lodge she should have fishing and camping experience herself," Ben counseled. "That way she can answer the travel agents' questions."

Matt nibbled his bottom lip. "That sounds plausible."

"Then take her out there the same way you would any tourist."

Well, yes, except that they'd share a tent. And a couple would zip their sleeping bags together. Oh, yes, the thought of them crowded in a two-man tent held plenty of appeal. Karen curled up against him in a double sleeping bag would be heaven after the frustrating nights he'd spent tossing and turning in his huge bed.

"You might have hit on something here," he murmured.

"Give it a try," Ben said, looking pleased with the outcome of their conversation. "I'd say let her do the cooking, though."

"But I generally do all that myself," Matt explained. When people paid him a thousand dollars or more for the

Alaska fishing experience, they didn't expect to have to fry up their own dinners.

"Women are really particular when it comes to that sort of thing," Ben explained. "They like to do their own cooking."

It had proved true so far, Matt thought. Karen had done all the cooking unless they had guests, in which case he took over.

"I think you might be right." Matt eased himself off the stool. "Thanks for everything."

"No problem," Ben and Sawyer said together as Matt left the café.

"DID YOU GET everything settled with Matt?" Scott asked Sawyer over dinner that evening.

"Settled?" Abbey looked from her husband to her son.

Scott stabbed his fork into the soft, pink flesh of fresh salmon. "Dad was advising Matt Caldwell about how to romance Karen."

"Sawyer was giving Matt advice? On romance?" Abbey wasn't sure what to think.

Sawyer grinned from ear to ear. "Yup. The poor guy came into Ben's all down in the mouth. No idea how to get back his ex-wife."

"And you told him?" This should be interesting.

"Yup." Sawyer made an exaggerated display of polishing his fingernails against the flannel sleeve of his shirt.

"You?" Abbey almost choked holding back a giggle.

"And Ben," Sawyer added defensively.

"They asked me a bunch of questions, too," Scott informed her.

"They asked you?" This was getting better by the minute.

Scott nodded.

"And what did you tell these three great romantics?" she asked her son. It took considerable restraint to keep the laughter out of her voice. Although she was deeply in love with Sawyer, the man knew as much about romance as she did about flying a plane. To his credit he tried, but she'd had to coax him every step of the way.

"I told Matt he should be affectionate," Scott said.

Sawyer frowned and with an air of superiority said, "Well, Scott, to my way of thinking, affection is something you give a dog. Women require a whole lot more."

"Is that right?" Abbey asked, and took a bite of her dinner in an effort to hide her smile. "What else?"

Scott's eyes narrowed as he concentrated. "Um, I told Matt to flatter Karen. Tell her how pretty she is and that kind of stuff."

"That's good."

"You think so?" Sawyer looked surprised. "We had a problem with that one."

"Oh?" This didn't come as a surprise to Abbey.

"Karen's got blue eyes and we couldn't think of something poetic to compare her eyes to."

"What about the sky?" Susan suggested, joining in the conversation.

"The sky," Sawyer repeated, pointing his fork at the eight-year-old. "I'll have to remember to tell Matt about that one."

Abbey rolled her eyes. "Just what did you three masters of romance finally suggest?"

Sawyer set aside his fork and planted his elbows on the table. He leaned forward as if he was about to share a wonderful secret.

"We're all ears," Abbey told her husband.

Sawyer spoke to the children. "Remember the time I took you and your mother to Abbey Lake?"

Both children nodded enthusiastically.

Sawyer beamed. "That's it."

"You mean you suggested Matt take Karen swimming?" Abbey remembered how cold the water had been, and the water fight that had ensued.

"Not swimming exactly," Sawyer said.

Abbey studied him expectantly.

"I thought the most romantic thing he could do was take Karen camping."

"Camping?" Abbey exploded.

"And fishing. Ben made a point of telling him he should let Karen do all the cooking, too. Women feel real proprietorial about those sorts of things," he added as though he was an expert on the subject.

"Oh, Sawyer," Abbey groaned, closing her eyes.

"Yup," he boasted. "That's what romance is all about. Taking a woman into the wilds, letting her share the wilderness experience."

Abbey buried her face in her hands.

"Great idea, don't you think?"

Abbey slowly shook her head. "Where, oh, where did I go wrong?"

CHAPTER SEVEN

"YOU KNOW WHAT I was just thinking?" Karen said over dinner. She studied Matt, who sat across the round oak table from her. Without guests, it made sense for them to dine in the kitchen, something they'd done all week.

Matt's look was absent, and he seemed absorbed in his own thoughts.

"Matt?"

"Sorry," he said, glancing up.

"I went over your books this afternoon." Karen half expected him to complain that his finances were none of her affair, and he'd be right. The lodge was his business, not hers.

"Did I make a mistake, mark the debits as credits?" he joked.

Matt would never make such an error, not after the months of training he'd received while working for one of Anchorage's largest accounting firms. "No, of course not."

The fact was, Matt was far more qualified than she to handle the books.

"I'm surprised at how well you're doing financially."

"It looks promising, doesn't it?" According to his reservation list, the dogsledding tours were booked solid. He'd collected a nonrefundable advance fee from each client. Karen was impressed with the way he'd handled the lodge's finances.

"You might think about hiring someone to help you this winter."

"Really?" Her suggestion appeared to surprise him. "You mean other than housekeeping?"

"Eventually you'll need some help in the kitchen and a couple more maids," Karen said. "And I was thinking you might want someone to pinch-hit for you with the winter tours." Since the baby was due in January, shortly before the first tour was scheduled, Karen was beginning to worry that Matt would be too busy to be with her. Although he'd arranged for professional mushers to train, supply and escort the participants, he'd be on the trail himself, hauling food, tents and other essentials. He'd be the one setting up camp each evening, cooking the meals, getting everything ready for the arrival of the dog teams.

"Why would I want to hire anyone just yet?"

Karen studied her stir-fry and pushed the green pea pods around her plate. How could the man not realize that the dates of his winter tours conflicted with her due date? She wanted Matt with her when the baby was born, but more than that, she wanted him to *want* to be with her. However, it wasn't something she would ask of him.

"No reason," she murmured, doing her best to hide her disappointment. "Looking over your ledgers, I thought you'd be able to afford to take on a couple of extra employees."

"I don't see why," he said without elaborating.

"Oh." Her appetite gone, Karen carried her plate to the sink. She stood with her back to him, collecting her composure.

Karen had done everything she could think of to push Matt out of her life. It shouldn't surprise her that he planned not to be available when she needed him. Maybe she should let him know how she felt, but the words stuck like a fish bone trapped in her throat.

"You sound disappointed," Matt said.

"No, no, the lodge is your business. It was a suggestion, that's all. Don't worry about it."

Later that evening, Karen was sitting on the porch knitting a blanket for the baby when Matt eased himself into the chair next to hers.

"I've been doing some thinking," he said.

"About what?" The knitting needles made soft clicking noises, and she jerked the string to unravel the soft pastel-green yarn.

"You've been taking a few phone reservations for the fishing tours lately."

"Yes." It surprised Karen how many people booked their vacations a year or more in advance. If the orders coming in for the following summer were any indication of what was to follow, Matt would be sold out before the end of the current year. She'd had no idea that people would be willing spend this kind of money to catch a few measly fish.

"I, uh, suspect there's been the occasional question you couldn't answer." He knew that to be true. More than once, she'd had to write down questions, ask Matt for the answers and then phone back.

"Yes," she said.

"It seems to me you'd be able to deal with that type of question better if you'd gone out on a fishing trip yourself."

"You want me to fly hundreds of miles from here to fish and camp so I can answer travel agents' questions?" That seemed a little extreme to her.

"Sure," Matt replied as though this made perfect sense to him. "You'll love it."

"We'll camp...in a *tent?*" Perhaps there was some other accommodation he hadn't told her about.

"It's the only way to go," Matt said, looking delighted with the idea.

"We'll cook over a camp stove?"

"You've never had better-tasting meals."

Karen didn't quite believe that.

"Come on, sweetheart, what do you say?"

She looked at him in shock. They'd been married four years and he apparently hadn't noticed she wasn't the camping type. She opened her mouth to tell him exactly what she thought, then stopped herself.

Matt was right. This was exactly the sort of thing she should do.

"If you agree we can leave in the morning," Matt coaxed, his eyes twinkling.

"Will we be gone one night or two?"

"Whatever you want."

"One night... You're sure you want to do this?" Karen didn't want to be difficult, but she did enjoy the more basic comforts.

"Of course I'm sure," Matt said, sounding a bit surprised. "We'll have a wonderful time, just you wait and see."

Karen would have been more than willing to wait. But she wanted to support Matt, and if that meant traipsing around the tundra, then she'd prove what a good sport she was by doing it.

MARIAH DOUGLAS waited for the paper to come out of the printer, then reread the letter she'd composed on Sawyer's behalf.

The phone rang and she reached for the receiver. "Midnight Sons. This is Mariah speaking. How may I help you?'' The static on the line told her it was a long-distance call.

"Mariah?"

"Tracy!"

She was thrilled to hear from Tracy Santiago. They'd become good friends and corresponded regularly. Tracy was the Seattle attorney Mariah's family had hired when they'd learned she'd accepted the position with Midnight Sons.

At the time there'd been a lot of publicity, some positive and some negative, about the O'Hallorans "luring" women north.

Although Mariah had repeatedly reassured her parents that everything was fine, they'd insisted on having the O'Hallorans investigated. They'd hired Tracy to fly up and check everything out. The attorney had asked a lot of questions, which made some people uneasy, and she'd inadvertently stirred up bad feelings. Mariah didn't blame her; Tracy was only doing her job.

Unfortunately Mariah had already started out on the wrong foot with one of her bosses—Christian O'Halloran. When Tracy showed up, the youngest O'Halloran brother held Mariah personally responsible and labeled her a troublemaker. From that day forward, he'd actively looked for an excuse to fire her. Mariah was certain she would've been laid off long before now if it hadn't been for Charles and Sawyer.

From that rocky beginning, things had quickly deteriorated. Lately her relationship with Christian was worse than usual. The incident at the wedding—when he'd spilled punch on himself—hadn't helped. He hadn't actually said so, but she knew he blamed her.

"I'm calling in an official capacity," Tracy explained. "It's been a year now, and your commitment to Midnight Sons is over."

"Yes, I know."

"Will you be moving back to Seattle?"

Mariah's family had probably put Tracy up to this. She didn't even consider the suggestion. In the past twelve months, she'd come to love Alaska and Hard Luck. For the first time in her life, she was out from under her family's dominance. She made her own decisions—and, consequently, her own mistakes.

"I'm staying right here," Mariah said.

"You're happy, then?" Tracy asked, sounding unsurprised, perhaps even a bit wistful.

"Very happy."

"What about the other women?"

"So far, everything's worked out just great. Mitch and Bethany were married this summer."

The door swung open, and Duke Porter walked into the mobile office. Mariah's gaze followed the bush pilot. She didn't know what it was about Tracy and Duke, but those two definitely rubbed each other the wrong way. Mariah had watched the sparks flash whenever they were together—and yet they each seemed to gravitate toward the other. It was an interesting phenomenon.

Personally Mariah liked Duke. True, he was a bit of a chauvinist, but a lot of what he said was simply for show. Or provocation. He'd toss out the most ridiculous comments just to rile everyone, then sit back and look pleased with himself. Tracy's problem was that she'd taken Duke at his word.

"I don't know if you remember Matt," Mariah said conversationally. "He's the one who bought the old lodge from the O'Hallorans. It's in full operation now, and his ex-wife, Karen, is back with him. Oh, and Abbey's pregnant. Karen, too. So how's everything with you, Tracy?" She purposely used the other woman's name, expecting a reaction from Duke.

He didn't disappoint her. No sooner had the lawyer's name left her lips when Duke wheeled around. "Is that highfalutin lawyer bugging you again?" he demanded.

"Just a minute, Tracy," Mariah said and held her hand over the mouthpiece. "Did you say something, Duke?"

"Is that Tracy Santiago?" he asked.

"Yes." Mariah nearly laughed out loud at the way fire seemed to ignite in Duke's eyes. Tracy was probably the only woman to ever challenge the laughable things Duke said and did. He didn't much like it.

Mariah always got a chuckle out of Duke's heated response to the lawyer. In fact, everyone laughed, but nevertheless, Mariah sensed that Duke and Tracy could be good friends if they'd only put their differences aside.

"What's she want?" Duke demanded.

"To talk to me," Mariah informed him sweetly, turning her back to him. "I'm here," she told Tracy.

Duke strolled purposely over to Mariah's desk in a blatant effort to catch what he could of the conversation. He didn't bother to hide his eavesdropping.

"Is that Duke Porter I hear?" Tracy's usually controlled voice went chilly.

"If you two ever made the effort, you might be friends," Mariah said to them both.

"I'd rather be friends with a skunk," Duke said loudly enough to be heard in Fairbanks.

"You tell Mr. Chauvinist I'd rather clean fish than have anything to do with him," Tracy snapped.

"Does she have a reason for calling or is she just hoping to stir up more trouble?" Duke asked, making sure Tracy heard that, as well.

"Mariah, listen, this doesn't sound like a good time for us to talk. Why don't you give me a call if you need anything." Tracy hesitated. "You know, I've come to think of you and the other women as my friends."

"You *are* a friend," Mariah assured her.

"With a friend like that, who needs—"

"Duke, enough," Mariah said, glaring at him.

"All right, all right," he muttered as he moved away from her desk.

"You'll keep in touch?" Tracy asked.

"Of course," Mariah promised. "Thanks for calling, Trace. It was good to hear from you."

She was about to replace the receiver when Tracy giggled and said, "Mariah?"

"Yeah?"

"Is Duke still there?"

"Yup."

Tracy giggled again. "Do something for me, would you?"

"Sure."

"Walk over to him and kiss him and tell him it's from me. Then ask if I'm still his favorite feminist."

Mariah grinned. "You're sure you want me to do this?"

"Positive. I just wish I could be there to see the look on his face when you tell him that kiss is from me."

"You got it," Mariah said, and she hung up the phone.

Duke studied her quizzically. "What was it she wanted this time?"

Mariah rolled back her chair. Her eyes on his, she stood and slowly made her way toward him. He was obviously uncomfortable with the way she'd focused her attention on him.

"Mariah?" Duke glanced around, then started moving backward as she continued her approach. He cleared his throat and glanced both ways. "What's the matter with you? You look like something out of *The Exorcist*."

"Tracy asked me to give you something," she said, making her voice low and sultry.

When Duke was backed right up to the wall, Mariah braced her hands on both sides of his face. Duke's eyes widened, and he opened his mouth to speak. He didn't get a chance.

Angling her head, Mariah planted her mouth firmly over his.

Duke squirmed.

Mariah heard the door open, but paid it no heed.

"Mariah!" Christian yelped. "Duke! What the hell is going on here?"

"YOU DIDN'T TELL ME my feet were going to get wet," Karen complained as they trudged along the marshy banks of the lake. Sawyer had delivered them by float plane to the same prime fishing area Matt brought his clients. The plane had taxied as close to the shore as possible, but they'd had to walk the rest of the way in. Through the water. No one had bothered to tell her this, Karen thought with some bitterness.

Something bit her and Karen slapped her neck. The mosquitoes swarming about her face were evidently thrilled with her arrival. Already she had two huge swellings on her neck. She'd be lucky to get out of this place whole at the rate the bugs were dining.

"If your feet are wet you'd better put on a fresh pair of shoes," Matt said after he finished unloading their supplies.

"I only have the one pair. You told me to pack light, remember?" If Sawyer was late picking them up the following afternoon, Karen swore she'd kill him. Her enthusiasm for this undertaking had never been high. The little interest she did feel was vanishing quickly.

"We'll make camp by that cluster of trees," Matt told her, pointing into the far distance. "The river's directly behind there."

Karen drew a deep breath as she remembered Lanni's adventure with the brown bear when she'd taken Abbey's children out to gather wildflowers on the tundra. Scott had delighted in telling Karen how he was sure they were about to become "dead meat" that afternoon.

Matt had tried to reassure her about bears, but she wasn't taking any chances. She'd had Mitch Harris teach her how to shoot off the can of pepper spray herself. Karen gave a heartfelt sigh. Matt seemed to believe this trek in the wilds would be one grand adventure. He'd talked excitedly about the wildlife they might see, mentioning moose, caribou, Dall sheep and wolves. Then he'd blithely told her she didn't have a thing to worry about.

"Why do mosquitoes love me so much?" she grumbled, although she didn't really expect an answer. "You'd think they were holding a dinner party and I was the main course."

"They're always more of a problem by the water," he reminded her.

Karen's feet made squishy sounds with every step she took. Matt might have advised her about adding an extra pair of shoes to her pack, she thought again—but she didn't want to be a complainer.

He was trying to make this a positive experience for her, and she felt guilty every time she found something else to gripe about. Unfortunately a camping-and-fishing trip wasn't even close to anything she considered fun. If Matt and his buddies enjoyed this kind of stuff, fine. Just leave her out of it.

"I brought along a bottle of wine," he said.

Good, Karen muttered to herself, she could use it for medicinal purposes; maybe dabbing it on her mosquito bites would relieve the itch. Had Matt forgotten she was pregnant and therefore wasn't drinking?

It seemed they'd been walking for miles, but in actuality, she realized, it couldn't have been more than a few hundred yards.

Matt slid the large backpack from his shoulder and set it on the ground. "We'll make camp here." Quickly and efficiently, he began to unpack.

He'd carried almost everything, and feeling equal parts guilt and exhaustion, Karen leaned against a large boulder and simply watched him.

"First I'll pitch the tent and then we'll do some fishing."

"What about dinner?" She was already hungry. It must have something to do with running around in the great outdoors, breathing fresh air. But then, you couldn't find air any purer than what she'd been breathing in good ol' Hard Luck. It seemed a crying shame to travel hundreds of miles north when the air at home was just as fresh and unpolluted. Besides, she could feel a cold coming on and would have preferred the comfort of her own surroundings. The truth was, she wouldn't mind crawling into bed right this minute. A *real* bed. *Her* bed.

"Dinner?" Matt said, his eyes twinkling with mischief. "That's why we're doing the fishing first."

Karen groaned. He honestly expected her to catch her own dinner. A crucial question occurred to her. Namely, what would she do if she struck out—did no fish mean no dinner? This was the first time she'd ever fished. Surely she should've taken lessons, gone to summer camp, something like that.

She felt decidedly annoyed that her very own ex-husband would assume she knew anything about this camping and fishing business when she'd never so much as baited a hook.

"It won't take me long to set up camp," he said, removing a few more things from the huge backpack.

Karen was astonished that he could carry everything they'd need for the night in that contraption. And she was impressed at how easily he assembled the small tent. Before she knew it, Matt stood in front of her, holding two fishing poles. "Ready?"

She wasn't. The new millennium could arrive, and she had the feeling she wouldn't be ready then, either. "I guess so," she said, forcing some enthusiasm into her voice.

It took effort to ease herself away from the rock.

Matt offered her his hand.

"I'm not good at this kind of thing," she muttered, slapping at another mosquito. Then she sneezed. Twice.

Matt led her to the river, whose rushing water emptied into the lake, and in no time Karen had a fishing pole in her hand. However, she soon learned that whatever it was that attracted fish—and she refused to believe it was the offensive-smelling egg at the end of her hook—she lacked it.

Clearly Matt didn't suffer the same affliction. He cast his line into the water and almost immediately got his first bite. He'd brought in two fish, one after the other, and all Karen had caught was a cold.

She sneezed once more and rubbed her nose with her sleeve.

Matt stood in the middle of the river—or "stream," as he called it—wearing rubber hip boots. Water swirled around him like a witch's caldron. He held his fishing pole in one hand and fed the line with the other. He glanced over at her and smiled in perfect contentment.

"It doesn't get any better than this!" He shouted over the sound of the surging water.

"You mean it gets worse?" she shouted back. Matt laughed; he seemed to think she was joking, but she was serious. Dead serious.

Uneasy about walking into the middle of a river, despite the protection of the hip boots Matt had given her, Karen remained close to shore, feeding her line into the clear, tumbling water. She'd about given up hope of snagging one of the rainbow trout that seemed to migrate toward Matt's line when she felt something nibble at her bait. She actually *felt* the fish nibble. Her eyes lit up, and she gasped with excitement.

"Matt." She didn't dare shout for fear of alerting the fish that it was about to become their main course. Matt didn't respond, so she raised her arm above her head and waved.

At that precise moment, the fish decided to take the bait and the fishing pole shot out of her hand.

"Matt!" she screamed, alerting him to what had happened.

"Grab that pole," he yelled, wading toward her, his eyes filled with panic. His expression told her she was replaceable, but the reel and rod were not.

Karen didn't have any choice but to go splashing into the fast-rushing stream after the rod. It would have been lost if the reel hadn't caught between two rocks. She just managed to rescue it, but lost her fish.

By the time she made her way back to shore, she was drenched.

Matt reached her side and jerked the pole away from her. "I thought I explained that this is expensive equipment! I can't afford to lose a rod and reel, so hold on to it, will you?"

She looked up at him and blinked back tears. When she spoke her voice sounded muffled—probably because she was struggling not to cry. Or sneeze. "I had a fish on the line. I . . . I wanted you to watch me bring it in."

He exhaled sharply, then placed his arm around her shoulders. "I'm sorry, honey. I shouldn't have yelled at you."

Karen sniffled, more than ready to abandon the whole venture, but Matt wouldn't hear of it. Against her will she was standing on the edge of the flowing water less than five minutes later. Sneezing. It seemed to take an eternity to attract another trout.

Soon, however, she experienced the same sense of exhilaration as a fish nibbled at her bait. This time she was ready when the trout encountered the hook. She gripped the fishing pole with both hands, prepared to catch a trout or die trying.

"That's it, honey!" Matt hollered, his excited voice carried on the wind. "Give the line more slack," he ordered.

Karen had no idea what he was talking about, but she must have done something right, because she didn't lose the fish. The muscles in her arms ached with the strain, but she held on as the fish leapt and fought.

Matt was there to lift her prize out of the water, using the net. "He's a beauty," her ex-husband told her with a proud grin.

"He sure is." Karen gazed at the fish fondly as he flopped around in the net.

Matt deftly removed the hook from the trout's mouth and was about to place it in the basket when Karen stopped him.

"Put him back," she said.

"Back?" Matt's eyes held a look that said he must have misunderstood her.

"He's too beautiful to eat. And too brave and noble."

"Karen . . . you're not serious."

"I mean it, Matt!" she cried. "I don't want him killed." Not after the way he'd struggled to live. Not after she'd looked him in the eye.

Matt did as she asked, but he wasn't pleased.

From that point forward their afternoon went downhill. Karen thought wryly that from her vantage point there was nowhere else for it to go. By dinnertime she was tired, hungry and in no mood to commune with nature. She wanted dinner, a hot bath and her own bed, in that order. No luck on any score, however.

Her contribution to dinner was a disaster. Fortunately, Matt had caught a couple of trout, which he cleaned while Karen prepared the vegetables. She dumped a can of beans into a pot, then sliced some potatoes to fry in a pan. By accident, she charred them. Smoke got in her eyes, blinding her, and she coughed and hacked. When she could actually see the potatoes again, they resembled dried cow chips. And the beans had become a mass of soggy lumps. To her relief, Matt took over then, and handled the frying of the fish. The result was delicious—even though Karen's misery didn't allow her to truly enjoy it.

Even Matt's festive mood had dissipated by the time they crawled into the tent that night. Tired as she was, Karen had assumed she'd immediately fall asleep. That wasn't the case.

For one thing the atmosphere in the tent was...intimate. If she'd understood that they were going to be holed up inside this tiny space together, she would have insisted they bring an additional tent.

"Something smells," she said after a few minutes. Every time she closed her eyes, her nose was assaulted by a repugnant scent. It reminded her of skunk.

"It's your mosquito lotion," Matt suggested.

"No, it isn't."

"It is, Karen. I've been smelling it on you all day."

"Fine." She rolled away from him, presenting him with her back. Just like a man to stink up a place and then claim it was the woman's fault. Anyway, if it *was* the bug repellent, which she doubted, he had it on, too. Maybe not as much as she did, but still...

Ten minutes must have passed before Matt spoke again. "I didn't mean that as an insult," he said gently.

"I know. I'm just tired and cranky." What she wouldn't give for a hot bath and clean sheets...

"You comfortable?" he asked next.

"No." She itched and her back hurt. Matt had placed an air mattress beneath the sleeping bag, but it was a poor substitute for a real bed. The ground was still hard.

Five minutes later she announced, "I've got to go to the bathroom."

"You just went half an hour ago," he reminded her.

"I can't help it. These things happen when a woman's pregnant. You don't need to come—I'm perfectly capable of marking my own territory."

Matt chuckled, but followed her out of the tent none-theless. When they crept back inside, the smell of the bug repellent wasn't as strong as it'd been earlier. Or maybe she'd just grown used to it.

Matt sprawled out atop the sleeping bag. He lay on his back, hands tucked behind his head.

Karen glanced at him, then released a slow, pent-up sigh and lay back down. She was careful to keep a respectable distance between them.

This wasn't so bad, she decided. It wasn't nearly as comfortable as the lodge, but she'd survive for one night. Barely. As long as they weren't attacked by any wildlife.

"Are you asleep?" Matt asked.

"No."

"Why don't you put your head on my shoulder?"

In other circumstances Karen might have worried that Matt was planning to seduce her. She doubted it now, though, since she wore half a bottle of bug repellent and hadn't bathed. Tentatively she rested her head on his shoulder and closed her eyes.

That felt better. A lot better.

"I'm a disappointment to you, aren't I?" she asked softly.

"No."

"I don't think I'm a good advertisement for the business. If any of the travel agents ask me about the fishing, I guess I can tell them about the one I set free."

Matt ran his hand along her hair. "You're doing okay."

"Well . . . I do have to confess this isn't my idea of a fun time."

"Really?" Matt seemed surprised.

"I'm sure plenty of women enjoy camping-and-fishing trips, but unfortunately I'm not one of them."

"But I thought—" He bit off the statement.

"What did you think?" she prodded.

He hesitated.

"Matt?"

"I thought . . . you'd consider this . . . romantic."

"Romantic?" The man was in need of therapy. Or maybe just a good dictionary.

"You said you wanted to be wooed."

"I do," she said, "but not like this."

Matt pulled away from her, raising himself up on one arm. Karen was unprepared for the sudden movement, and her head hit the hard ground.

"Ouch." Her eyes smarted. She rubbed the back of her head.

"Why isn't this romantic?" Matt demanded.

"You honestly have to ask?" She made a sweeping gesture with one hand. "My feet have developed jungle rot. I've been the main course and every other course for the entire mosquito population. Then you set me next to the Hoover Dam and when I nearly lose your precious rod and reel, you make it clear that the damn thing's worth more than I am!"

"I'll have you know that reel cost five hundred dollars."

Karen gasped at the news, but it didn't slow her down. *"Then* you insist I cook dinner, probably to punish me because I had the audacity to set free a beautiful, brave trout who deserved to live."

"Oh, please."

"And you call this romantic?" she sat up, crossing her arms in a huff. "I call it torture."

The silence fell like a landslide between them.

"All right," Matt said after an awkward few minutes. "We got off to a bad start. I'll do better next time."

"Next time?" There was more?

"You wanted wooing, didn't you?" He had the nerve to sound angry. "And wooing means romance, right?"

"Right."

"Then that's what you're getting."

"Wouldn't it be easier," she said between clenched teeth, "to torture me on a rack? At this rate I don't know how much longer I'll survive."

CHAPTER EIGHT

"Just look at me," Karen told Lanni, holding out her bare arms for inspection. A number of red, swollen mosquito bites marked her pale skin. "The bugs ate me alive."

Lanni walked over to the library table where Abbey kept the newest hardcover releases. She chose a murder mystery Duke Porter had returned earlier that afternoon. "Are you telling me you didn't have a good time?"

Karen shrugged, not sure how to answer her friend, who also happened to be Matt's sister. She realized she was placing Lanni in an uncomfortable position by asking her to side against her own brother.

"I had the experience of a lifetime—and I've never been more miserable." Karen sighed heavily and made a dismissive gesture. "I didn't mean to put you on the spot. It's just that this whole fishing business has left me flustered. And cranky." She sighed again. "Matt seemed to think he was doing me a favor."

Karen began to look through the library books, grateful for an excuse to get away from the lodge. Matt had been sullen and uncommunicative ever since they'd returned. Granted, she hadn't exactly been cheerful herself. She didn't understand how two people who clearly loved each other could find themselves at odds over something as ridiculous as a fishing trip. Matt had been trying to share his vision of the future. And she'd...well, she'd been looking for a way to survive a night in the wilderness.

"It may not have been the vacation of your dreams," Lanni commented, "but now you'll be able to answer any questions the travel agents ask, won't you?"

"I'm convinced that was just a ploy Matt used to get me to come with him," Karen muttered. "His sole purpose in all this was to romance me, if you can believe it."

Abbey returned just then, carrying a tray filled with tea things from the library kitchen. "I'm afraid Sawyer and Ben are to blame for that," she said, setting the tray down on the desk.

"What do those two have to do with this?" Karen wanted to know.

As she poured them each a cup of tea, Abbey said, "Apparently Matt decided to, uh, seek their advice on how to win you back."

"Ben and Sawyer?" Lanni cried. "Why, Ben's never been married!"

"I know," Abbey said, making an effort to conceal a smile and failing. "Frankly Sawyer isn't much better when it comes to being romantic. He tries, but I'm afraid he was a bachelor for far too many years. I planned to warn you, but one thing led to another, and before I realized it you and Matt had already left."

"He dragged me into the wilds in the name of romance." Karen shook her head. How could Matt possibly have believed she'd consider it romantic to traipse around for two days in wet shoes, with mosquitoes, the threat of bears and no hot water?

"I'm crazy in love with Charles," Lanni said, "and I do happen to like camping. Nothing romantic about it, though. In fact, I can safely say Charles knows as much about romance as Matt. In other words, nothing."

"What man really does?" Abbey asked as she handed around a plate of homemade cookies to accompany the tea.

Karen shook her head. "I guess I was asking the impossible when I suggested Matt woo me. Instead, he's woed me." She chuckled at her own witticism.

Both of the other women laughed, too.

"When we were first married," Abbey said, "I could see that this romance business was going to be a problem. I love Sawyer so much—he's a good man, a wonderful husband and father. I guess women are more sentimental than men. We occasionally want a symbol or an expression of love. I mean, I want him to realize there are certain dates that are important to me—dates I want him to remember. Not that I expect anything extravagant. The price of the gift isn't important."

Karen and Lanni nodded in agreement.

"It's the thought that goes into it," Karen added for good measure. "And knowing that he cares enough to make the effort. No woman likes to be taken for granted."

"Exactly," Abbey said.

"What dates did you give him?" Lanni asked. "That is, if you don't mind my prying."

"Not at all." Abbey stirred a spoonful of sugar into her tea. "I explained to Sawyer that Valentine Day, my birthday, our anniversary and Christmas were important to me. I asked that he remember me on those days." Her gaze grew soft and warm. "He said there wasn't a chance on this green earth that he'd forget me any day of his life—which was sweet, but not the point."

"How'd you clue him in on buying you a gift?" Karen asked.

"Actually Scott was the one who told him that when I said I wanted to be remembered I was really saying he should buy me something."

"What did Sawyer say to that?"

Abbey grinned. "He took out a pen and a piece of paper and wrote down all the dates, then tucked it in his wallet."

"So, has he remembered?" Lanni asked eagerly. "You know, this is good advice."

"Yeah, he has." Abbey grinned widely. "He's never had to buy a woman presents before—apart from his mother— so he generally seeks advice from the kids."

"Scott and Susan?" Karen couldn't suppress a laugh.

"I know. At least my husband had the sense to realize I wouldn't be interested in Barbie's Playhouse or a new computer game. For my birthday this year he bought me a cookbook about homemade bread."

"Not bad," Karen said, impressed. She recalled that for her birthday the last year she and Matt were married, he'd bought her a lens for his camera.

"It *was* a thoughtful gesture," Abbey agreed, "but he had an ulterior motive. He was mostly interested in having fresh-baked bread," Abbey explained. "Like his mother used to make."

"What did he give you on Valentine Day?" Lanni asked.

Abbey sipped from her tea. "He wasn't very imaginative. He bought me a box of chocolates and then promptly picked out his favorites."

"Matt mailed me a card for Valentine Day," Karen murmured, remembering how keenly the simple card had affected her. She'd dug it out of the garbage and kept it, too.

"I know why he did," Lanni told her. "At least I think I do. You sent a Christmas card for Matt last year, along with your gifts to the family, remember?"

Karen wasn't likely to forget. She'd agonized over that card. She hadn't wanted to ignore him, but at the same time, she didn't feel it would be a good idea to encourage him to think there was any possibility of a reconciliation. He'd never mentioned the card, or said anything about the note she'd sent with it. She wondered if he'd kept it, the way she had his valentine message.

The valentine card was meant to be a reminder that he still loved her and wanted her with him, she suspected. It had come when she was most vulnerable, when she'd been trying her hardest to put Matt and their marriage behind her. As if she could *ever* forget Matt, no matter how hard she tried.

"What's going to happen between you and my brother?" Lanni asked, her expression serious. "Will you really go back to California after the baby's born?"

Karen didn't know how to answer that. "I don't know... I want us to make a new start together. Heaven knows I love him enough, but we still have some things to work out."

"He's trying," Lanni reminded her.

Karen scratched at the mosquito bites on her arms. "I'm afraid if he tries any harder it'll do me in."

CHARLES WAS READING a scientific journal when he heard someone on the porch. Setting aside the magazine, he walked into the living room, half expecting Lanni's return from the library.

To his surprise his visitor was his youngest brother. "Well, hello, Christian. Come on in."

"Thanks." Christian stepped inside and glanced around. "Where's Lanni?"

"Over at the library."

Christian seemed relieved. "I hope I'm not disturbing you," he said, with an uneasiness that wasn't like him.

"Not at all. Can I get you anything?"

"Yeah," Christian said stiffly. "A new secretary."

Charles didn't bother to conceal his impatience. "What's the matter with Mariah?"

"We don't get along," he spat out. He sank onto the sofa. "I don't know what's wrong, but I don't like the woman. Never have."

"What does Sawyer think?"

Christian shrugged. "He doesn't seem to have a problem with her, and since we went to the expense of flying her up to Alaska, he isn't that keen on firing her."

"So you've come to me, hoping I'd talk Sawyer into agreeing with you."

Christian's eyes brightened. "Yes," he blurted, and then shook his head. "No. Hell, I don't know what I want. Yes, I do. I want Mariah out of that office. If she chooses to stay in Hard Luck, fine. As far as I'm concerned, she has as much right to stay here as anyone else."

"What about employment?"

A pained expression came over Christian's face. "Ben's been talking about hiring some help."

"But Mariah's not a waitress."

Christian rubbed a hand along the back of his neck. Charles could tell he'd given the matter thought. "Matt will need to take on an employee or two at some point. Let him deal with her. Just get her out of my sight."

Charles mulled this over, unsure how to respond. "It could be some time before Matt can afford to take on an employee. It wouldn't surprise me if Karen decides to stay after the baby's born. That'll mean extra expenses—and an extra person to help out at the lodge. Karen's already filling a lot of the gaps. Do you honestly think Mariah can afford to wait around till Matt's ready to hire her?''

"No.'' Christian frowned. "The hell if I know what to do with her. There's got to be somewhere she can go. I wish Sawyer and I could agree on this.''

Charles sat on a chair across from his brother, gazing down at his feet. He was reluctant to involve himself in areas like hiring—and firing. Although he was a full partner with his two brothers in Midnight Sons, he was a silent one. Generally he left these types of decisions to Sawyer and Christian.

"Has Mariah made expensive mistakes?'' he asked, buying time to consider the situation. Charles couldn't remember ever seeing Christian this flustered. That he'd sought him out for advice said quite a bit.

It took Christian several long moments to answer. "Mistakes,'' he finally repeated. "She made plenty of those in the beginning, but she seems to manage everything adequately enough now.''

If the increase in profits was an indication, the woman had been a godsend, Charles mused. She'd skillfully organized the office and developed a system of rotation for the pilots that they considered fair. That was something Sawyer and Christian had never managed to accomplish. Mariah had even started an advertising program that had attracted new business. But Charles didn't think Christian would appreciate his singing Mariah's praises.

"Her year's up,'' Christian pointed out. With a deepening scowl, he said, "She's fulfilled her contractual obligation. The property and the cabin are legally hers.''

"But you'd prefer it if she left.''

"No," Christian muttered, then almost as if he wasn't aware he was speaking, added, "She spilled punch down the front of my suit at Mitch and Bethany's reception."

"The way I heard it you were as much to blame for that as she was."

Christian didn't respond, apparently caught up in his own thoughts. "I've reviewed a number of the applications I took last year, and there's another woman I'd like to invite up here."

"To take Mariah's job?"

"Yes," Christian admitted. "You probably don't remember, but I never intended to hire Mariah. I wanted Allison Reynolds."

"Who?"

"You never met Allison. She flew up and only stayed one night, but she was perfect, Charles. I took one look at her and... well..." He shook his head. "That no longer matters."

"Then how'd you happen to hire Mariah?"

Christian stood and walked around the living room, pausing in front of the fireplace. "As I said, Allison left after a...short stay. I was discouraged, so I reached for the first application on the top of the pile. In retrospect, I'm fairly sure I didn't read it."

"But you phoned and asked Mariah if she wanted the job?"

"Yeah. I didn't even remember who she was. I can't be expected to recall every person in every interview, can I?"

"No, I suppose not."

"Mariah's the one responsible for that lawyer snooping around, asking questions." Christian seemed to be looking for excuses to get rid of her.

"I know," Charles said. But in his opinion, Tracy Santiago had been a blessing in disguise. Without realizing what they were doing, his brothers had set themselves up for trouble with this scheme of theirs. Tracy Santiago had opened their eyes to the legal problems they'd invited with this venture. Luckily, as it turned out, any women who might have created serious difficulties for them had quickly moved on.

"You're sure firing her is what you want?" Charles asked, sympathetic to both sides. He liked and respected Mariah, but he'd known for a long while that Christian didn't get along with her. He was also aware that it could be damned uncomfortable to work with someone who was a constant source of irritation, for whatever reason.

The intense look in his brother's eyes revealed just how uncomfortable he was. "I don't know," he muttered. "I just don't know."

"Can you figure out what it is about Mariah that bothers you so much?" Charles asked, hoping Christian could come up with a solution of his own.

"That's the crux of the matter," Christian confessed. "When everything's said and done, Mariah's turned out to be a pretty decent secretary. The truth is, I simply don't want to be around her."

His brother was one contradiction after another.

"Never mind," Christian said with a deep sigh. "I have a feeling the problem will take care of itself, anyway."

Now Charles was confused. "What do you mean?"

"I think Duke's going to marry her."

"Duke?"

"Yeah, I found the two of them kissing the other day."

"Duke and Mariah?" Charles couldn't picture it.

"That's what I said," Christian snapped.

"You're sure?"

"I happened on them myself. This isn't hearsay, Charlie. I saw them kissing with my own two eyes."

Charles scratched the side of his head as he struggled to visualize them as a couple. Certainly stranger things had happened. Lanni had fallen in love with him, hadn't she? Heaven knew, she could have had any man she wanted. That she fell in love with him struck Charles even now as nothing short of incredible—but a blessing he wasn't about to question.

"Forget we had this conversation." Christian sounded eager to be on his way. "I suspect I just needed a sounding board and you were handy."

"Fine. I've wiped it from my memory."

"Good." Christian was at the door. "I don't begrudge them happiness, you know."

"Who?"

Christian cast a baffled glance at Charles on his way out the door. "Mariah and Duke. Who else?"

"Right," Charles called after him. He stood in the open doorway and watched his youngest brother head off down the dirt road. Charles recognized that woebegone look. The first time he'd seen it, Sawyer had it plastered all over his face. Abbey was about to leave Hard Luck and Sawyer was beside himself, wondering how he could persuade her and the kids to stay.

Charles knew he'd worn that look himself the afternoon he discovered Lanni was Catherine Fletcher's granddaughter. It had felt as if his entire world had come crashing down.

Now that same look was in Christian's eyes. Charles chuckled, almost pitying his brother. Christian didn't have a clue what was about to hit him.

MATT STEPPED into the Hard Luck Café and let the screen door slam in his wake. He didn't walk up to the counter the way he usually did, but stared out the window at the airfield. John Henderson was picking up guests for the lodge, two retired college professors, who'd taken the afternoon flight into Fairbanks. John and company were due at Hard Luck within ten minutes.

"You want any coffee?" Ben called from behind the counter.

"No, but I'd like a refund for the last cup."

"A refund? What the hell for? I make the best coffee in town and you know it." Ben sounded insulted.

"The coffee was fine, but the advice stunk."

Ben chuckled, but Matt didn't find this at all amusing. He should have known better than to take advice on romance from a confirmed bachelor. And Sawyer hadn't been much better. Matt didn't know what the hell he'd been thinking; he'd been desperate, he decided. Desperate enough to seek the counsel of two men who were as ignorant in the ways of women as he was himself.

With guests at the lodge, Matt feared his relationship with Karen would become even more strained. He'd genuinely wanted her to enjoy their camping-and-fishing adventure. What he'd hoped, he admitted now, was that she'd be so impressed with him and his operation here she'd throw her arms around his neck, declare how much she loved him and promise never to leave him again.

Instead, they were barely on speaking terms.

Matt's intention had been to romance her, but he'd consider himself fortunate if she didn't pack up and return to California by the end of the week.

"I guess things didn't work out the way you wanted," Ben said.

At least the old coot had the good grace to sound contrite. "You could say that. Now on top of everything else, Karen's furious with me because she got a couple of bug bites and because her feet were wet for two days."

Ben chuckled, and if the situation hadn't been so critical, Matt was sure he would've seen the humor in it himself.

"Did she catch any fish?" Ben asked.

"One." Matt still had trouble believing Karen had set the trout free. Leave it to a woman to assign human characteristics to a fish. Brave and noble. For crying out loud, she was talking about a trout. A trout! Karen looked at this fish and saw a poor, maligned creature of God. Matt looked at the same fish and saw dinner.

If that two-day trek in the wilds was any indication of how their relationship was going, Matt might as well give up now.

"I take it you've got guests flying in."

"A couple of college professors," Matt explained, his thoughts still on Karen. He hadn't seen her since early that morning. He'd gotten everything ready for the evening meal himself, then spent the remainder of the day gathering the necessary supplies for the trip. He'd be away three days this time. He'd venture a guess that Karen would be pleased to have him gone. His biggest fear was that she'd leave before he returned.

He wished he could find a way to settle their differences once and for all, but every attempt he made seemed to backfire.

EARLY THAT EVENING, as the four of them sat down for dinner in the lodge dining room, Matt felt torn. Despite his natural sociability, he would've liked nothing better than to spend a quiet evening with his wife; he wanted a chance to right any wrong he'd unintentionally committed against her.

Unfortunately he found himself reluctantly sitting across the table from the two white-haired professors—likable though they were—and chatting with them. Both men, Donald and Derrick, were in their early sixties and full of vigor. They'd apparently been friends for years and often traveled together. One was married, the other divorced. They talked freely about their lives in a relaxed, companionable way.

Karen was her usual gracious self throughout the meal. She asked a question now and then in that thoughtful way of hers and listened intently to the answer. She was a perfect hostess, making their guests feel interesting, valued, important. It was her gift, one that had touched him from the first moment they'd met.

"I hope Matt had you sign the guest book," Karen said as she passed around the basket of fresh-baked rolls. They were still warm from the oven.

"I had them sign it first thing," Matt answered on their behalf, since both were busy eating.

"I understand this is your first season operating the lodge," Donald, the more animated of the two, said after a moment.

"That's right."

"We're still pretty new at this," Karen added.

"So far, it's been a delightful experience," Derrick said, smiling at Karen. "I must say, Mrs. Caldwell, dinner is delicious."

"Thank you, but I can't accept the credit. Matt's the chef at the lodge."

"The grilled salmon is excellent," Donald told him.

Matt shrugged off the compliment. "Thanks," he said gruffly.

"I'd be interested in knowing your background," Derrick said conversationally. "It seems to me you must be a jack-of-all-trades."

"And a master of none," Matt said, completing the old saying. "Actually that pretty well sizes up the situation. I've dabbled in a number of careers in the past few years."

"When I first met Matt he was a psychology major," Karen explained, avoiding meeting his eyes.

"Did you graduate?" Derrick directed the question to Matt.

"No." If he was uncomfortable with compliments, he was even more uncomfortable discussing the twists and turns his life had taken since college.

"He knows just enough about human nature to make him dangerous," Karen teased affectionately.

Matt couldn't take his eyes off his ex-wife. She looked radiant that evening. He wondered if she was ready to put their differences behind them. He knew *he* was. He hoped that if he got down on his knees and promised never to take her camping again, she'd be willing to forget and forgive. If she wanted romance he'd find some other method of providing it. He didn't know what, but he'd figure it out.

"You're an excellent cook, as well," Donald was saying.

"At one point in my illustrious past I decided I wanted to cook. That was soon after Karen and I were married." He saw no need to mention that they were currently divorced.

"Matt developed a number of excellent recipes and an extensive repertoire," Karen said.

It actually sounded as though Karen was boasting, but Matt was sure he was mistaken. He remembered how furious she'd been the day he'd announced he didn't want to be a chef, after all. When he'd finished his course at a culinary institute, he'd been hired as a sous-chef by a major hotel. The job had allowed for no creative freedom, and after ten months, Matt felt that his inventiveness had been stifled to the point that he could barely stand going into work.

Karen hadn't been pleased when he'd quit, but she'd supported his decision. That was when he'd decided to become a commercial fisherman and had hired on with a fishing vessel. The money was good—no, great—but the dangers were high. Fishing some of the roughest seas in the world was risky, and a number of vessels were lost every year.

"Not exactly," Matt said, and glanced toward Karen. This conversation had become disquieting. The last thing Matt wanted was to have his lack of direction discussed and dissected by his guests. It had always been such a contentious issue between him and Karen. He didn't want her to recite the litany of his failings. Not now when he was struggling to get back into her good graces.

"After leaving cooking school Matt decided to become a commercial fisherman," she announced.

"Where'd you fish?" Once more the question was directed to him.

"The Bering Straits," Matt answered with little enthusiasm. His gaze briefly met Karen's and he realized she was thinking the same thing he was. Those months apart while he'd been at sea had been some of the most difficult in their marriage.

Sure, the money had helped them meet their bills, but it hadn't been worth the strain on their marriage.

"How long did you fish commercially?" Donald asked.

"One season." He didn't elaborate, didn't say that when he'd first gone into the trade he'd dreamed of one day owning his own boat. But then, he'd also fantasized about running his own restaurant.

Although he was sure Karen would deny it, he'd given up fishing for her. She'd worried herself sick the entire time he was at sea, and Matt realized he couldn't do that to her. So he'd left at the end of the season and joined an accounting firm.

"After that Matt worked for an accountant—for a while," Karen said.

"Accounting," Derrick echoed. "My, but you have led a varied life."

"It's interesting to note how everything has pulled together for you now," Donald said thoughtfully. He helped himself to seconds of the salmon and while he was at it reached for another roll.

Matt looked at him curiously.

"You're happy with the lodge?" Donald asked.

"Perfectly happy." Matt said this as much for Karen's benefit as to answer the question.

"Yes, it's all pulled together for you now," Donald repeated. He had everyone's attention.

"How do you mean?" Karen pressed. She made it sound as though Matt couldn't be trusted not to sell the lodge at the drop of a hat. Not that he would've blamed her. He'd certainly given her enough grief with his erratic work history during their marriage.

"You were interested in psychology first, isn't that right?" Donald asked.

"Yes," Matt murmured, wondering how their conversation could have veered so far off course.

"Then cooking school?"

"Yes." Karen was the one to answer this time.

"For which he shows remarkable talent." Another dinner roll disappeared.

"Followed by a stint as a commercial fisherman," Donald went on.

"One season was all," Matt insisted. He'd tried to mak‹ that clear in his arguments with Karen. While the fishing had been adventurous and lucrative, it hadn't been a rea‹ career.

"Followed by accounting."

"Nine months' worth." Again it was Karen who sup plied the details. "And now the lodge."

"This lodge means everything to me," Matt said. H‹ yearned to explain that he'd invested his entire trust fun‹ in the venture, rebuilt the place with his own two hand and was personally involved with every phase of its oper ation.

The professors exchanged looks.

"If anyone were to design a course on opening a lodge I'm convinced they'd follow this exact same pattern," Donald said. "It's as if everything you've done in the pas five or six years has steered you in this direction. I predic that Hard Luck Lodge is destined to be a success."

"You have a basic understanding of human nature," Derrick added. "Naturally Donald and I came up for th fishing, but if you continue to feed us meals like this, we' certainly be coming back—even if we don't catch a thing.'

Both men chuckled. "The fact that you've fished con mercially is bound to be an asset."

"True," Matt admitted.

"Plus your accounting experience."

"It's a perfect fit." Donald nodded with evident satis faction.

"Thank you," Matt said. Funny, he'd never realized a this before. The two men were absolutely right. It was a though he'd spent the past years in training for this ver thing.

"If you gentlemen would kindly excuse me?" Unex pectedly Karen stood up.

"By all means." The professors rose politely to their feet and thanked her for her hospitality.

She threw them a quick smile and rushed into the kitchen.

Matt didn't know what was wrong, but knew he'd better find out. He decided he'd give her a couple of minutes, then excuse himself from the table, too.

Fortunately the professors made some comment about heading up to bed, since they'd spent the better part of the day traveling. Matt waited until they were on their way up the stairs, then hurried into the kitchen.

"Karen, what's wrong—" He'd no sooner walked through the door when Karen hurled a wet sponge at him. It stuck to his shirt.

"What was that for?" he asked, stunned.

CHAPTER NINE

"KAREN," MATT WHISPERED, approaching her slowly.

She reached for the next-closest item at hand, which happened to be half a head of lettuce. "Stay away from me, Matthew Caldwell." Her cheeks were streaked with tears.

"Why are you so upset?"

She flung the lettuce at him, but Matt ducked in the nick of time. Not that she really wanted to hit him. She wasn't sure *what* she wanted to do.

"Karen?"

She couldn't bear it when he said her name like that. As if she was the most precious, the most beautiful woman on the face of the earth. As if he'd treasure her until eternity.

"I'm warning you—stay away from me." She backed up, edging toward the door, hoping to make a clean escape. If she got past him, she'd run up the stairs and flee to the haven of her room. Then, and only then, would she try to analyze the reason for her tears. She experienced a confusing mix of emotions—anger, guilt and a sudden, overpowering sadness that she could neither define nor explain.

"Tell me what's upsetting you," he pleaded.

"I can't." She shook her head helplessly; she didn't understand it herself. She didn't know *why* she felt so furious, or where to direct her anger.

But everything was somehow linked to their dinner conversation. The two professors had taken the apparent chaos that had ruled her marriage and Matt's life and seemed to find logic in it. Karen had been blinded by her complete lack of faith in her husband. A problem, she suspected, that was a result of her childhood.

"Why can't you explain?" he coaxed.

"Just leave me alone, Matt Caldwell," she wailed.

"No." His stubborn streak was showing. "You know I can't stand to see you cry."

"Then I'll stop." She sniffled hard in an effort to stem the tears. Matt wasn't the only one upset with her crying; it troubled her, too. Karen *hated* to cry. It made her nose red and runny, it made her eyes puffy and, worst of all, it made her weak. Vulnerable. Whenever she wept she wanted to be held. When they were married, it was Matt who held her. His comforting often led to lovemaking, which only complicated the issues between them.

Matt stretched out his arms to her. "Honey, let's talk about this."

She wavered, the lure of his embrace strong. It demanded every ounce of fortitude she possessed to shake her head. She was at the kitchen wall now, easing her way toward the door.

"Karen, I love you so damned much."

She pressed her hands over her ears. "Don't tell me that," she sobbed.

"Why not?" he demanded. "Don't you know by now that I'd move heaven and earth to have you back? I want you and our baby here, with me. I want us married."

"You only want me because of the baby."

"That's not true," he argued vehemently. "Do you know any other man who'd have agreed to live the way we do? Damn it, Karen, I'm going crazy. Do you think it's been easy living with you day after day, loving you the way I do and not touching you? We hardly even kiss.''

"We can't kiss," she mumbled. Kissing was always the beginning for them; the lovemaking rarely stopped there.

"If you want to be angry with me, fine, but let me at least hold you.''

That was generally the way their fights went. She'd be unhappy over something that Matt found trivial and unimportant, and she'd explode. She'd usually throw things, and in an effort to calm her, Matt would comfort her. The comforting led to kissing and the kissing to much more. She didn't want it to happen that way now.

"No," she said. "Not again. You seem to forget I'm not your wife any longer.''

"The hell you aren't," Matt growled. "Sure, you've got some judge's decree in your hot little hands, but that doesn't change the way I think of you. You're my wife as much tonight as you were the day we married. I never understood this whole divorce business. You're the one who wanted it, but are you happy?''

She couldn't answer. Besides, he already knew. She'd divorced him, moved to California—and had never been more miserable in her life.

Removing herself from the temptation of being close to Matt simply hadn't worked. Here, she was, pregnant with his child, living with him. Difficult as this was to admit, she was happier than she'd been in two years. And it infuriated her.

The tears came in earnest then.

"Karen, for heaven's sake . . .''

She hadn't the energy to run from him, and she slumped against the wall. In giant strides, Matt crossed the kitchen and gathered her in his arms. "Honey, listen, nothing can be that terrible.''

"Yes, it can," she sobbed, hiding her face in her hands.

The warm feel of his body pressing her against the wall seeped into her bones, chasing away the chill that centered in her heart. Karen could feel his breath at her temple, gently mussing her hair.

She didn't know who reached out first; it didn't matter. She was as hungry for him, as needy for her husband, as he was for her. His touch no longer merely comforted but excited. His lips were warm as they covered her mouth. His tongue traced her lips, then explored with eager thrusts. Soon their need for each other was consuming them.

"Matt, oh, Matt..." She breathed his name again and again as he buried his face in her neck. She slid her arms around him and pressed her body against his solid strength.

"I've been crazy for you for weeks," he muttered, whisking open the buttons of her blouse. Her breasts peaked, yearning for his touch. "But I'll be damned if I'll make love to you in the kitchen."

"Do you think this is such a good idea?" she asked as Matt swung her up in his arms. He opened the swinging door with a push of his shoulder and carried her past the registration desk and toward his private quarters.

"Our making love is a brilliant idea," he said, walking past the dining-room table.

"Matt, the dishes," she said, pointing.

"To hell with the dishes."

"You're angry." She was always the one who flew off the handle. Not Matt.

"Not angry," he corrected, "frustrated with this foolishness. I want my wife back."

She looped her arms around his neck and kissed him hungrily. His eyes met hers briefly before his strides took them into his darkened bedroom. His eyes filled with tenderness as he placed her gently on the mattress and knelt over her. "You asked for romance. I swear I'd do anything in the world to give it to you if I could only figure out what the hell it is," he said before he kissed her again.

"You seem to be doing a pretty good job at the moment," she whispered, her arms looped around his neck.

"I am?" He sounded both surprised and pleased.

"But I still think we should talk first."

"Not on your life," he said, removing her shoes and carelessly tossing them aside. He kicked off his own. "Not when there's a chance you might change your mind about us making love."

"I . . . I promised myself we wouldn't."

"You can unpromise yourself just as easily."

Karen held out her arms to him in open invitation. "I guess I'll have to."

WHEN KAREN AWOKE it was still dark. The space beside her on the bed was empty. "Matt," she whispered, sitting up and clutching the sheet to her chest. She saw his shadowy figure in the dim light and realized he was dressing.

"Is it morning already?" she asked, yawning luxuriously.

"Unfortunately, yes." He sat on the edge of the bed. "I've got to get the professors up and fed before Sawyer flies us out."

"You're leaving?" She'd completely forgotten about the professors and that Matt would be taking them fishing. "But we need to talk," she said urgently.

"It'll have to wait until later. I'm sorry, honey, but I don't have any choice."

"How long do we have to wait?"

"Three days," he told her. "Besides, what's there to discuss? Everything's already settled, isn't it? You're moving into this bedroom with me and we're getting married again as soon as I can arrange it."

"Aren't you taking a lot for granted?" she asked, piqued that he'd assume everything was settled simply because they'd made love. She wanted to right their relationship, remarry him, too. But contrary to Matt's assertion, there remained a great deal to discuss.

"You love me. I love you. There's nothing more to be said."

"Listen to me, Matthew Caldwell, we have to clear the air. We need to—"

"I don't have time, honey," he said. "Hold that thought and I'll be back in three days."

Discouraged, Karen fell back against the pillows and exhaled sharply.

Nothing was settled, although thanks to what the two professors had pointed out, Karen had a far better understanding of Matt, of their history and his ambitions for the lodge . . . and of her own reactions the night before.

The professors were right, but neither she nor Matt had seen the obvious. He'd found his calling, had unconsciously been working toward this for as long as she'd known him. The lodge wasn't another phase; it was his life's work. And it had taken two strangers to make both Matt and her aware of that.

Now Karen understood the reason for her tears the night before—they'd been prompted by both anger and sadness. And, she had to admit, guilt. She hadn't trusted Matt to find his own way, to find the work that suited him. She'd allowed her mother's experience to cloud her judgment. Her fears and insecurities had controlled her life, and she'd suffered because of it. Not only had she brought grief into her own life, but into Matt's, as well.

LANNI STOOD at the kitchen sink staring unseeingly at the world outside the window. Her thoughts were troubled as she reviewed her conversation with Karen the day before.

Charles stepped up behind her and slipped his arms around her waist. "You're thoughtful this morning," he said, kissing her neck. "Is something bothering you?"

"It's Matt and Karen," Lanni murmured. She set aside her cup and turned to wrap her arms around her husband, hugging him close. "Something's happened between them."

"Good or bad?"

"I don't know," Lanni confessed. She closed her eyes and savored the feel of Charles's arms. When Matt and Karen had separated she'd been careful not to take sides. Karen was one of her best friends, but Matt was a brother she idolized.

Following the divorce, she knew he was feeling lost and confused. In retrospect, Lanni wished she'd been more sympathetic. Karen's leaving him had undermined the very foundation of his life.

"I saw Karen, but where's Matt?" Charles asked, breaking into her thoughts.

"He's off doing his wilderness thing." Lanni leaned her head back far enough to look into her husband's eyes. "I couldn't bear to ever lose you," she said fervently, offering him a blurry smile.

Charles stroked her back lovingly. "What brought that on?"

"I was just thinking about my brother and Karen. When Karen left him and filed for divorce, it was as if someone had pulled the rug out from under him. He was miserable.

"Yet when I saw Karen soon after they'd separated, I realized she was just as heartbroken. I couldn't take sides or interfere—at least I didn't feel I could—and now I wonder if that was a mistake.''

Charles kissed the top of her head. "What I hear you asking, oh, wife of mine, is whether you should involve yourself now.''

"Yes.'' It astonished Lanni that Charles understood her so well. Until he'd spoken, she wasn't sure exactly where her thoughts were leading. "That is what I'm wondering. My brother's a private person, and I don't think he'd appreciate my meddling in his affairs, but at the same time...'' She hesitated.

"What makes you think you should?''

"I was over to see Karen yesterday,'' Lanni said, then bit her lower lip. "I knew Matt was gone, and I thought I'd pop in and see how she was doing. At first everything was fine. We chatted and laughed the way we normally do, and then out of the blue Karen started to cry.''

"Karen? About what?''

"That's the sixty-four thousand dollar question,'' Lanni said, more confused now than ever. "When I asked her what was wrong, she shook her head, hugged me and told me I was the best friend she'd ever had.''

"Hmm.''

"What's 'hmm' mean?''

"Nothing,'' Charles answered. "Do you think this bout of melancholy is related to her pregnancy? I've heard a woman's emotions sometimes go a little screwy with a pregnancy.''

"How would I know? I've never been pregnant.''

She felt Charles smile against her hair. "Not from lack of trying.''

"Stop, Charles. We're talking about Matt and Karen here, not my insatiable appetite for my husband.''

"Being that husband, I should mention how grateful I am for a loving wife."

"That's just it," Lanni said urgently. "Can you imagine how awful it would be if something were ever to drive us apart?"

The smile in her husband's eyes faded. "I couldn't bear it, Lanni. Loving you has changed my life for the better in so many ways. It's transformed everything. For the first time I have a healthy relationship with my mother. I have you to thank for that. Even the way I feel toward my brothers is different because of you."

Charles dropped his arms and pulled out a kitchen chair and sat down heavily. "I remember when I learned that Sawyer and Christian had brought women to Hard Luck. I was furious. Then I talked to Abbey and discovered my two brothers had expected her and those children to live in one of those old cabins. I was outraged. I decided to put an immediate end to this ridiculous idea of theirs."

Lanni pulled out a chair for herself and sat opposite him. "Don't forget about those twenty acres the women were promised."

He snickered at that, but the amusement soon faded. "I was the one who suggested Abbey leave Hard Luck. When Sawyer heard what I'd done, the most incredible look came over him. It was as if I'd stabbed him in the back, betrayed him. Then he told me something I've never forgotten."

"What did he say?" Lanni asked when he didn't continue right away.

"Sawyer told me I was tempting the fates with my arrogance. He'd never expected to fall in love, and if it happened to him, then I was just as vulnerable. Someday I was going to fall in love myself, and he hoped he'd be there to see it, because then and only then would I appreciate wha he was feeling." Charles laughed softly and shook his head. "Not long after that I met you, and I felt I'd been smacked upside the head with a two-by-four."

"I felt the same way after meeting you," she said.

Charles reached for her hand and kissed her fingertips.

"Remember how Matt tried to bring us back together?" Lanni asked.

Charles nodded.

"I can understand now why he did something so uncharacteristic." Her throat seemed to close and she blinked back tears at the memory. "He was hoping to spare us the same kind of heartache he was suffering."

"Now you want to help him?"

"Yes," Lanni said fervently. "But I don't know how, and I'm afraid that if I say or do something it might hurt more than it helps."

"I don't know what to tell you, sweetheart."

"I just wish I knew what to do."

"Perhaps if you talked it over with another woman," he suggested. "Someone you trust and respect."

Lanni's eyes brightened; she leapt out of the chair and planted a grateful kiss on his lips. "You mean someone like Abbey."

FAT RAINDROPS plopped down on the dirt road. Karen studied the pattern they made on the hard ground as she leaned against the support beam on the lodge porch.

She wrapped her arms around her waist and gazed up at the dark, angry sky. Matt and the professors weren't due back until the following day. In her loneliness it felt like an eternity.

Scott O'Halloran came racing down the road on his bicycle, with Ronny Gold behind him. Their young legs pumped the pedals furiously. Eagle Catcher easily kept pace with the two boys, staying closest to Scott's side.

Scott saw Karen and slammed on his brakes. "Hi, Mrs. Caldwell."

"Hello, Scott."

"Do you have a name for your baby yet?" he wanted to know.

"Not yet," she told him. "Do you have any suggestions?"

Scott pinched his lips as he mulled over the question. Then, with a look of excitement, he suggested, "Scott's a good name."

"So's Ronny," the other boy shouted.

"I'll keep both of those in mind," she assured them. "Don't you think you should get out of the rain?"

"Nah," Scott said, answering for them both. "I used to live in Seattle. I'm used to this sort of thing. Once you've lived in the Pacific Northwest, you learn to take rain in your stride."

"I'll remember that," she said, smiling a little at his grown-up manner.

"Look," Ronny said, tugging at the sleeve of Scott's jacket. "The girls are right behind us. We gotta split."

"'Bye," Scott said, arching forward over the handlebars in an effort to make a fast getaway.

Chrissie Harris and Susan O'Halloran raced after them. "Hello, Mrs. Caldwell!" Chrissie shouted.

"Hello, Chrissie. Hello, Susan."

Susan gave her a swift wave and paused only briefly, saying, "Scott let Ronny read my journal, and he's gonna pay."

"You're sure your brother would do something like that?" Karen asked, not quite concealing a smile.

"I'm sure," Susan said with righteous indignation.

"Ronny wrote her a note in the margin of the page. Boys," Chrissie Harris said with wide-eyed wisdom, "are not to be trusted." The two girls disappeared, chasing after the boys.

Now for the first time it came to Karen that this Hard Luck was a good town to raise her child. Although the town was small, the sense of family and community was strong.

She knew there were occasional problems. Friday nights when Ben served alcohol, some of the local trappers and pipeline workers drifted into town and every now and again a fight broke out. But Mitch was routinely there to take care of things.

Karen remained on the porch, musing about life in Hard Luck, when Abbey strolled past, carrying an umbrella.

"Howdy, neighbor," her friend called.

When Karen returned her greeting Sawyer's wife stopped and studied her carefully. "How're you feeling?"

"Fine." She was, if a little lonely. She missed Matt and wished he was home. Her heart was full of all the things she wanted to tell him.

Abbey moved onto the porch. "Do you have time to sit and chat for a while?"

"Sure." Karen was grateful for the company.

They sat side by side on the porch steps. "So how's life treating you these days?" her friend asked.

Karen rolled her shoulders in a shrug. "I can't complain." But she could. In truth, Karen felt wretched, although her condition wasn't physical. The malady was one of the heart.

Tears filled her eyes, and she knew Abbey saw her struggle to keep them at bay. She was thankful that her friend didn't comment or ply her with questions. Instead, Abbey gave her a moment to compose herself.

"I imagine the lodge must feel empty when Matt's away," Abbey said in a quiet, conversational tone.

"It does." Days like this made Karen wonder how she'd managed without Matt during their year and a half apart. In her first months of pregnancy, she'd felt alone and afraid, and the harder she'd tried to convince herself she didn't need Matt, the less it became true. She did need him. The fact that she'd been tempted to keep the baby a secret from him proved as much—she'd been fighting the very thing she wanted most. It seemed to be a pattern in her life.

"I've been feeling so blue lately," Karen admitted softly.

Abbey reached for her hand and squeezed it. "Sounds to me like you could use a little cheering up."

Karen managed a watery smile. "What do you have in mind?"

Abbey gave her a knowing smile in return. "What does every woman do when the going gets tough?"

"Shop," Karen answered automatically.

"Sawyer's flying into Fairbanks later today. Why don't you and I tag along and check out baby furniture? It's time the two of us indulged ourselves at a real, live shopping mall."

"That," Karen said, brightening immediately, "is an offer too good to refuse."

MATT HAD NEVER in his life been so eager to head home. Good thing he wasn't responsible for the weather, because it had rained for two days solid, and there was no letup in sight. Donald and Derrick, his two clients, had called a halt to their expedition. They were wet, cold and miserable.

Luckily the fishing had been great, and the two men felt they'd gotten more than their money's worth. What they wanted now was a hot bath, a good dinner and a warm bed.

Matt was in complete agreement. He radioed in to Midnight Sons and requested that Sawyer fly out and pick them up a day early. Unfortunately Sawyer was in Fairbanks, but Christian agreed to meet them. It might have been Matt's imagination, but Christian sounded eager to get out of the office.

Although the weather was dismal, that wasn't the only reason Matt felt eager to get home. He missed Karen. He wanted to be with her, hold her, make plans for the future. The last thing he wanted to do was discuss the past. It seemed to him that a lot of their problems had come as a result of these discussions. He'd always dreaded it when she wanted to clear the air, because those conversations invariably led to more problems between them. He never understood why women found it necessary to dissect every aspect of a relationship.

As far as he was concerned, the matter of Karen and him being together was simple. He loved her. He wanted her and the baby with him. If she didn't want that, too, well...

But Matt knew Karen. A man couldn't live with a woman for more than four years and not become well acquainted with her ways. She loved him so damned much it hurt. He knew that in the very depths of his heart. *She loved him.* What bothered Matt was her reason for holding out.

All right, he understood that his tendency to drift from one kind of job to another had troubled her. But all of that was tied to her childhood and her father.

Matt wasn't anything like Eric Rocklin, and if Karen hadn't figured that out by now, he thought with a spurt of anger, then she never would.

Christian arrived in the float plane late in the afternoon. It took the two of them more than an hour to load up the gear. Matt sat next to him in the copilot seat and watched as the landscape unfurled below them and the town of Hard Luck finally appeared. A swelling sense of pride filled him as the lodge came into view.

But it wasn't only the lodge that beckoned him. His wife would be there, and for the first time in a long while he felt like a husband again.

It seemed to take forever to reach the lodge. He imagined Karen rushing out to greet him, and the anticipation set his heart racing. He could hardly wait to take her in his arms again. They had a lot of lost time to make up for.

"Karen!" he shouted as he pushed open the heavy wooden door and strode through. "I'm home."

The two bedraggled professors followed close on his heels.

"Karen!" he repeated, louder this time.

No response.

"She must have gone out," he explained to the two men. The image of her rushing to greet him crumbled at his feet.

Donald and Derrick mumbled something about a bath and immediately headed up the stairs.

Matt wandered through the house, looking for his ex-wife. It wasn't as if she was expecting him; nevertheless, he felt a deep sense of disappointment that she wasn't home.

When she hadn't returned an hour later, he called the library. To his surprise his sister answered.

"I don't suppose you've seen Karen?" he asked without preamble.

"Not today," she told him, and it seemed to him that she stopped herself from saying more.

"Do you know where she might be?" he probed.

Lanni hesitated. "I haven't got a clue. Let me check around and see what I can find out for you."

"I'd appreciate it." He hung up and, because he didn't have any choice, he started the dinner preparations.

Peeling potatoes, he thought about his short conversation with his sister. It suddenly occurred to him that something wasn't right. Wedging the receiver between his shoulder and ear, he punched out the number for the library.

"What's going on with Karen?" He wanted the truth, and he wanted it now.

"What do you mean?" she asked.

"You're keeping something from me."

"I—" Lanni stopped.

"Tell me," he ordered.

"Something's happened between you two, hasn't it?" his sister asked.

"Yes," he said, but to his way of thinking, the changes were all good. She was back in his bed, and as soon as he could make the arrangements, they'd get remarried.

"Whatever it was must have really upset Karen," Lanni said gently.

"What do you mean?" he demanded. He'd thought, he'd hoped, that Karen would be excited. That she'd be happy. He realized she wanted to "clear the air,"—have one of those discussions he disliked so much—but he'd assumed they'd scaled the major hurdles by admitting how much they loved each other and wanted to be together.

"When I stopped by to see Karen she started crying for no reason."

"Crying? Just where the hell is she?" he asked, losing his patience.

"If you'd give me a chance I'd tell you," Lanni snapped. "I talked to Scott, and he told me Karen flew into Fairbanks with Abbey and Sawyer. They're due back anytime now, so don't worry."

By ten that night it became clear that Karen had no intention of returning.

She'd left him again.

Well, it wasn't the first time, but it as sure as hell would be the last.

CHAPTER TEN

ABBEY WAS RIGHT. A shopping spree in Fairbanks had done wonders for Karen's spirits. Sawyer had dropped the two of them off at the closest mall and arranged a time to meet them later.

Karen and Abbey had delighted in drifting from one store to another, from one baby department to the next. Karen felt like a child let loose in Toyland at Christmas.

The experience of shopping for baby clothes had produced a flood of tenderness for her unborn child. Choosing sleepers and nighties somehow made everything more immediate, made the baby seem *real*. Before she could stop herself she bought a number of things, almost more than she could carry comfortably. She put a crib and changing table on layaway and selected several other items for a layette.

The most fun she had was trying on maternity clothes with Abbey. Karen hadn't laughed this much in ages. The smocks were huge on her. But although she barely showed, she could no longer button her pants. Abbey was an old pro at this pregnancy business, and she assured Karen that before long, those smocks would be a perfect fit.

Sawyer met them at the scheduled time, and because of the rainstorm, suggested dinner in Fairbanks before flying back to Hard Luck. When they finally landed that evening it was after ten. The afternoon away had been the perfect remedy for her case of the blues. Karen felt happy—and exhausted.

Sawyer and Abbey dropped her off at the lodge. Sawyer climbed out of the truck, helped her down and sorted through the packages before handing Karen her purchases.

"Looks like someone's inside," Abbey said, gesturing toward the front window where a light showed in the growing dusk.

"Do you think Matt might be back?" Sawyer asked.

"I doubt it," Karen answered. Knowing her ex-husband, he'd probably consider the rain and wind something of a bonus. She'd heard it said that rain made for good fishing, but then, what she knew about the sport was minimal. She could imagine Matt standing in the middle of a raging river that very minute, happily soaked and hoping to lure breakfast toward his hook.

"Thanks again," Karen called as her friends drove off. She shifted the sacks in her arms, pleased with the things she'd purchased and looking forward to showing Matt.

"One thing's for sure," she said aloud to the baby, "whether you're a boy or a girl, you're going to be one of the best-dressed kids around."

She suddenly realized that she and Matt had never talked about the baby's sex. She didn't know if he had any preference; he'd never said.

No sooner was she inside than her eyes connected with those of her ex-husband. He was sprawled in the overstuffed chair in front of the fireplace. His feet were propped on the raised hearth and his outstretched arms dangled over the sides of the chair. One hand was holding the neck of a whiskey bottle, which seemed in danger of slipping from his fingers.

"Karen?" He stared at her as though she were an apparition.

"You're back early!" she said excitedly. "This is a surprise."

"You can say that again."

She ignored the sarcasm in his voice. "I've had the most marvelous day." Hurrying across the room, she set down her packages in the empty chair. "Just wait until you see what I bought the baby!"

He continued to stare at her. Although the liquor bottle appeared to be nearly full, Karen wondered how much Matt had been drinking. It wasn't like him to overindulge. As she recalled, he was easily hung over and generally avoided the hard stuff. He was more inclined to drink wine, but rarely to excess.

"Why are you buying these things now?" he asked in a snarling tone.

"Because I had the opportunity to fly into Fairbanks with Sawyer and Abbey," she explained with strained patience. Surely he wasn't upset because she'd bought things for the baby. Ignoring his sour mood, she pulled a yellow cotton sleeper from the sack. "Isn't this adorable? You wouldn't believe the incredible things they have for babies these days. I found the cutest pair of baby sunglasses. Abbey and I got a real kick out of them. You can flip up the lenses and everything."

"Baby sunglasses," he muttered, but he didn't sound impressed.

It was clear that her ex-husband—soon to be husband again—was in a rare temper. Karen lowered herself onto the hearth, facing him. "What happened?" she asked with a laborious sigh.

After the long, happy afternoon she was tired and disappointed by his lack of welcome. The last thing she wanted now was a confrontation with Matt. "Didn't the professors have a good time? Are they demanding their money back?"

"Hell, no," Matt said irritably, obviously taking offense at the question. "They had the time of their lives and made a point of telling me so. They would have stuck it out if the rain hadn't started coming down in buckets."

"So that's why you came back a day early?"

His eyes narrowed as he glared at her. "I surprised you, didn't I?" He set the bottle aside and stood, looming above her. She noticed that his balance was a little off, and he braced his feet wide apart in an effort to maintain it. "You figured to be out of here by then, didn't you?" he went on. "You were planning to be gone before I learned what you'd done."

"Out of here? Gone?" Karen had thought they'd be able to sit down and discuss where their lives were headed, how their relationship would change. But she had no intention of leaving him. It was the furthest thing from her mind.

"Sure," he said with more than a hint of belligerence. "You intended to sneak out of Hard Luck without telling me."

"You assumed because I wasn't here when you returned that I'd *left* you?" This was by far the most ridiculous thing he'd ever said. She leapt to her feet and stuffed the yellow sleeper back into the bag.

"What else was I to think?"

"If you'd bothered to look in your office you'd have found a note."

"You wrote me a note when I wasn't expected home?" he challenged, his eyes bright with disbelief.

"You or anyone else who happened to stop by and wanted to know where I was." She held the packages tightly against her stomach as if to protect herself from Matt's hostility. This wasn't like him; she didn't understand it, didn't know how to respond.

"You left me before," he reminded her. "What else am I to think when I return home and find you gone?"

"That was different," she said in her defense.

His short laugh was devoid of amusement. "The last time, you filed for divorce so fast you left my head spinning. Remember? You couldn't wait to be rid of me then. Nothing's changed. Certainly not you."

Karen almost gasped with pain at his accusation. Her knees felt weak, but she stood her ground. "I warned you, Matt, but you wouldn't listen. You hardly ever listened to me in those days." He didn't seem to have improved much now.

"You warned me?" he spat out.

Karen glanced over her shoulder and up the stairs, fearing his outburst would wake their guests. Well, so be it, if that was what Matt wanted.

"When you decided to become an accountant I told you to be very sure. You'd already gone through three other professions in short order, and I wasn't about to have you risk our financial security again."

"To be very sure is a long way from filing divorce papers," he said sullenly.

"You didn't even discuss it with me. I come home from work one night and you gleefully announce that you've quit." Tears threatened, but she held them back with sheer force of will. "Without a word of warning, without so much as hinting you were unhappy, you quit. If you'd once talked to me, explained that the job wasn't right for you... But you left me completely out of the decision."

"And so the next day you packed up your bags and were gone," he said. He snapped his fingers as if to say her leaving had been a snap decision.

"Can you blame me?" she cried. "Can you honestly blame me? I was tired of having you jerk our lives around. I'd had it up to here," she said, raising her hand above her head, "with your inability to stick to a job. Any job." She paused and dragged in a deep breath before she continued, "I'd grown up with a father who refused to accept responsibility. Then I'd made the mistake of marrying a man just like him."

"I am not your father." Matt made each word loud and distinct.

"You're exactly like him. You didn't even think about the bills. They were supposed to pay themselves, I guess. Your 'Don't worry, be happy' attitude drove me *crazy*."

"I was miserable working for the accounting firm!" he shouted.

"Just as you were miserable continuing with college, with the chef's job, with commercial fishing and with everything else you dabbled in over the past five years? Or was this a *different* kind of misery?"

He didn't answer.

"The time had come to grow up, Matt. You didn't want a family, you drifted from job to job, without revealing an ounce of responsibility or any ambition, any plan for our future. What else was I supposed to do?"

"Answer me this, Karen. Would a responsible adult turn tail at the first sign of trouble? Would a responsible adult walk out on her husband and end her marriage on a whim?"

"Do you really think that was easy for me, Matt?" Her voice shook as she stiffened against his accusations.

"Easy or not, you did it, and I don't trust you not to look for some excuse to do it again."

"Is that what the bottle's all about?" she demanded, pointing to the whiskey in his hand.

"Yes. I returned early and you were gone. When I called around all I could find out was that you'd been feeling low. Then I discovered you'd gone into Fairbanks with Sawyer and Abbey."

"For heaven's sake, I went shopping!"

"I didn't know that. For all I knew, you could be returning to that wonderful job in California that you love so damned much."

She couldn't believe what she was hearing. It hurt that he was saying such things. "Why would I do that?"

He shrugged. "Why do you do anything? What happened two years ago makes as little sense to me now as it did then."

"You're being ridiculous."

"Am I?" he challenged. "The last thing you said to me before I left the other day was that I shouldn't take you for granted. Trust me, Karen, I don't. I never will again. You're as likely to walk out on me now as you were before, and I can't—I *won't*—forget that."

"Just because I didn't leap back into marriage when I learned I was pregnant? As far as I could see—"

Matt didn't allow her to finish. "If you're going to go, Karen, I advise you to do it now. I haven't got the stomach to drink away my sorrows. Nor do I enjoy living with uncertainty."

"You honestly believe I'd do anything so underhand?"

"Why shouldn't I? You did it before."

She swallowed at the constriction blocking her throat. "Fine, then, I will." She moved toward the stairs. "You didn't need an excuse to get me to leave, Matt. All you had to do was ask.''

MARIAH WAS HUMMING to herself when Duke Porter opened the office door and walked in. She looked up, relieved to find it wasn't Christian. Her boss appeared to be doing his utmost to avoid her these days. Which was just as well.

"Hello, Duke." She greeted him with a cheerful smile.

Duke stayed close to the door, as if he was ready to make a quick exit. "If I come in here you aren't going to kiss me again, are you?"

Mariah laughed. "A lot of guys around here wouldn't complain if I did."

"Maybe not," Duke agreed good-naturedly, "but you said the kiss was from that attorney friend of yours. Tracy something or other."

"It was." Duke wasn't fooling her; he knew Tracy's name as well as he did his own. He should—he'd been complaining about her for months.

Duke rubbed the back of his hand across his lips as if to wipe away anything having to do with the lawyer. "Let me set one thing straight right now. The last woman I want kissing me is that . . . that she-devil."

"She's not so bad."

"She wouldn't be if she knew her place."

"Knew her place?" Mariah echoed in disbelief. "What do you mean by that?"

"Exactly what I said." He walked over to the coffee-pot, removed his mug from the peg and poured himself a cup. "She thinks just because she's an attorney, she knows better than anyone else. What that woman needs is a man to put her in her place."

Mariah opened her mouth in outrage, then felt a laugh gurgling up. Duke went out of his way to be provocative, and frankly she'd like to see him or any other man try to put Tracy in "her place." She didn't know what it was with those two. They hadn't gotten along from the very first moment they'd encountered each other.

Suddenly dejected, Mariah realized it had been that way with her and Christian, too. The first day she arrived in Hard Luck her suitcases had fallen open and her unmentionables had scattered across the runway. That beginning must have been an omen. Things had quickly gone from bad to worse between them. The man flustered her so much she'd made one mistake after another.

"Speaking of Tracy," Mariah said, forcefully taking her mind off Christian, "I received a letter from her this week."

"Oh." Duke sat on the edge of her desk. "She's not making a trip up here, I hope."

"She's got two weeks' vacation due her, and she wanted to know if I'd meet her somewhere."

"Like where?"

"I was thinking of Anchorage. I've always wanted to go on one of those glacier tour boats." She opened a bottom drawer and removed a brochure. "There's plenty I'd like to see in Anchorage, especially Earthquake Park. It's supposed to be quite something."

"Any chance you might invite her up here again?"

"Here?" She eyed the pilot, wondering if he was hoping to stir up a little trouble. Mariah sometimes thought Duke was attracted to Tracy, but she dismissed the idea. Not Duke and Tracy. Not the two people who couldn't exchange one civil word.

"Maybe I will," she said, studying him.

Duke scowled. "In that case let me know so I can avoid her. I don't want to be within a two-hundred-mile radius of her."

He sipped his coffee, grimaced as if he found it not to his liking and walked out of the office.

No more than a minute later the office door opened again. Without looking up she chided, "Come on, Duke. Make up your mind, would you? You—" She stopped abruptly when she did look up and saw not Duke, but Christian.

His gaze focused on her. "Was that Duke I noticed coming out of here? Or should I say loverboy?"

"Yes," she answered stiffly. "It was Duke." Judging by his expression, Christian seemed to be suggesting that she and Duke had been involved in something unseemly. "And for your information, Duke isn't my loverboy."

"The two of you were in here alone?"

"Yes." She rolled her eyes and sat down at the computer, presenting him with a view of her back. It did no good to reason with Christian. He'd already decided she and Duke were romantically involved, and he seemed unwilling to change his mind.

"Do you think that's such a good idea?" he asked.

"What? Being in here alone with Duke? Really, Christian, he's a pilot. It isn't like he doesn't have business here." She was about to point out that she was the one who scheduled the flights, took orders and handled numerous other details, but she realized her arguments were useless.

"The last time I caught the two of you together you were practically undressing one another."

"That's not true!" Mariah's cheeks reddened with embarrassment. "You make it sound like I need a . . . a babysitter."

"You do," Christian sneered. "It's a miracle you haven't destroyed the airfield by now. You certainly have a habit of wreaking havoc wherever you go."

"That's the most unfair and unkind thing you've ever said to me, Christian O'Halloran." Pride demanded she hold her head high, but it was difficult.

Mariah had known for a long time that Christian regretted hiring her. She was also aware that he'd approached Sawyer soon after her arrival, wanting to replace her. If anything, his dislike for her had spurred her on; she'd tried harder to please him, to fit into the office and prove herself. She'd hoped that in the past year she'd done that.

She had worked hard. When it came to Sawyer she had a near-flawless record. But with Christian everything had gone wrong. Spilling punch on him was just the tip of the iceberg. If she lost an important file it was inevitably one Christian needed. If she misplaced a phone message it was one Christian had been anxiously waiting to receive. It never failed; she was continually in conflict with him, when he was the very one she most wanted to please.

For nearly a year Mariah had lived with the threat of losing her job. Just when it seemed they were making progress and finding some common ground, Christian had stumbled on her kissing Duke. Everything had gone downhill since.

He avoided her whenever possible. When it wasn't possible and they were in the office alone at the same time, he rarely spoke to her, and then only about business. It made for an awkward situation, and Mariah didn't know what to do to change the situation for the better.

KAREN'S SUITCASES were packed and ready to be taken to the airfield. The two professors had left earlier that morning, and the lodge was strangely quiet.

Karen had been downstairs only once all morning; Matt wasn't there. Now she waited in her room, although for what she wasn't sure.

The tightness in her chest hadn't gone away from the moment she announced she was leaving. The phone call to her parents in Anchorage had assured her she was welcome to live with them as long as she needed.

She walked over to her window and stared out at the panoramic view of the tundra. She would miss all this. More important, she'd miss the friends she'd made here. Lanni, of course. Abbey and the children. Bethany, and although she didn't know Mitch well, she thought the world of his little girl. Then there was Ben. And the O'Halloran brothers. Duke and John and Ted, and the other pilots.

But she was fooling herself, Karen knew, if she believed it was the townsfolk she'd miss most. For the second time in her life she was about to walk away from the man she loved.

It had been difficult enough the first time. She didn't know if she could find the strength do it again.

A noise echoed up the stairway from below. The screen door slammed, indicating Matt was back.

Leaving her suitcases at the top of the stairs, Karen slowly made her way down.

Matt stood at the foot of the stairs watching her.

Neither spoke.

His eyes seemed huge, twice their normal size. It took Karen a moment to realize that the tears brimming in her own eyes had distorted his image.

"Are you ready to leave?" he asked starkly.

"No," she answered. Her fingers tightened around the railing. All at once, in a rush of pain, Karen knew she'd never be ready. She couldn't make herself do it. She couldn't leave him. Not again.

Her gaze scanned the room. During dinner the night before in Fairbanks Sawyer and Abbey had told her how hard Matt had worked to rebuild the lodge. How he'd taken on an impossible task and made this half-burned, abandoned place a promising enterprise. How pleased they were to have her and Matt as part of the community. They'd spoken of Hard Luck's future, and Karen had felt a vital part of that future. Until she'd arrived home. Until she'd faced Matt.

The moment she'd moved into the lodge with him she'd seen it all for herself. He'd found his calling. Everything he'd done in the last few years had steered him in this direction. The professors had revealed that truth to her. A truth that should have been obvious. All she'd had to do was watch her husband here in his lodge. His capability, the care he took, the responsibilities he assumed—they all should have told her that things were different for him now.

In all the time she and Matt had been married, she'd never seen him this happy, with himself or his work.

"What do you need?" he demanded.

"Need?"

"To get ready to leave."

It seemed he couldn't be rid of her fast enough. She didn't know how to answer him and glanced behind her.

"I'll get your suitcases," he said, and he took the stairs two at a time, roaring past her.

"No." The word nearly strangled her.

He stopped midway up the stairs. "No?"

"I don't want to leave you, Matt," she choked out. "Not again. The baby needs you. *I* need you."

A strained silence followed.

"How long?" he asked, his voice taut with emotion. "How long are you willing to stay this time?"

"Forever."

A deep breath of air filled his chest. "I don't know if forever will be long enough. Are you certain Karen? Be very certain because I won't have the strength to let you go again if that's what you want."

"I *am* sure," she said, and the tears ran down her face.

All at once they were wrapped in each other's arms. Matt was kissing her and she was crying and kissing him back.

They both tried to speak a number of times, but it seemed more important to reassure each other with kisses.

"Never again," Matt whispered between kisses.

"No. I'm here for a lifetime."

"Partner. Lover. Companion," Matt said between nibbling kisses.

"I am moving," she whispered, and laughed at the way his eyes lit up like fire, "into your bedroom."

"*Our* bedroom. I remodeled that room with you in mind."

"What about a family?"

"That, too," he agreed, smiling.

Tears of happiness sparkled on her lashes. "I have so many ideas for the lodge."

"Wonderful." He pressed his mouth hungrily to hers.

"But I have an even better idea for right now."

He lifted his head and his gaze probed hers. "You do?"

"It doesn't have a thing to do with the lodge, either." Gripping his hand, she led him down the stairs and toward their private quarters.

"Might I ask what you have in mind?"

She laughed joyously. "You'll find out soon enough, oh, husband of mine."

*   *   *   *   *   *

Mariah and Christian—is there any hope for romance here? For love? Find out in FALLING FOR HIM, *the fifth book in Debbie Macomber's* MIDNIGHT SONS.

BRIDE'S
BAY RESORT

UNLOCK THE DOOR TO GREAT ROMANCE
AT BRIDE'S BAY RESORT

Join Harlequin's new across-the-lines series, set
in an exclusive hotel on an island off the coast of
South Carolina.

Seven of your favorite authors will bring you exciting stories
about fascinating heroes and heroines discovering love at
Bride's Bay Resort.

Look for these fabulous stories coming to a store near you
beginning in January 1996.

Harlequin American Romance #613 in January
Matchmaking Baby by Cathy Gillen Thacker

Harlequin Presents #1794 in February
Indiscretions by Robyn Donald

Harlequin Intrigue #362 in March
Love and Lies by Dawn Stewardson

Harlequin Romance #3404 in April
Make Believe Engagement by Day Leclaire

Harlequin Temptation #588 in May
Stranger in the Night by Roseanne Williams

Harlequin Superromance #695 in June
Married to a Stranger by Connie Bennett

Harlequin Historicals #324 in July
Dulcie's Gift by Ruth Langan

Visit Bride's Bay Resort each month wherever
Harlequin books are sold.

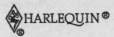

HARLEQUIN ®

BBAYG

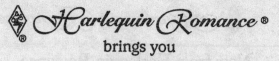

Harlequin Romance ®

brings you

How the West was Wooed!

We've rounded up twelve of our most popular authors, and the result is a whole year of romance, Western style. Every month we'll be bringing you a spirited, independent woman whose heart is about to be lassoed by a rugged, handsome, one-hundred-percent cowboy! Watch for...

- March: **CLANTON'S WOMAN**—Patricia Knoll
- April: **A DANGEROUS MAGIC**—Patricia Wilson
- May: **THE BADLANDS BRIDE**—Rebecca Winters
- June: **RUNAWAY WEDDING**—Ruth Jean Dale
- July: **A RANCH, A RING AND EVERYTHING**—Val Daniels

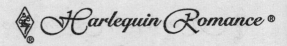

Harlequin Romance ®

New from Harlequin Romance
a very special six-book series by

MIDNIGHT SONS

DEBBIE MACOMBER

The town of Hard Luck, Alaska, needs women!

The O'Halloran brothers, who run a bush-plane service
called **Midnight Sons**, are heading a campaign to
attract women to Hard Luck. *(Location: north of the
Arctic Circle. Population: 150—mostly men!)*

"Debbie Macomber's *Midnight Sons* series is a delightful
romantic saga. And each book is a powerful, engaging story
in its own right. Unforgettable!"
                                              —Linda Lael Miller

TITLE IN THE MIDNIGHT SONS SERIES:

DMS-1

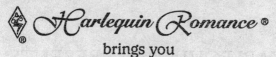

HARLEQUIN PRESENTS®

Harlequin brings you the best books, by the best authors!

ANNE MATHER

"...her own special brand of enchantment."
—*Affaire de Coeur*

&

LINDSAY ARMSTRONG

"...commands the reader's attention."
—*Romantic Times*

Next month:

A WOMAN OF PASSION by Anne Mather
Harlequin Presents #1797

Ice maiden...or sensuous seductress? Only Matthew Aitken
guessed that Helen's cool exterior hid her passionate
nature...*but* wasn't he already involved with Fleur—who just
happened to be Helen's mother!

TRIAL BY MARRIAGE by Lindsay Armstrong
Harlequin Presents #1798

To outsiders Sarah seemed like a typical
spinster schoolteacher.

Cliff Wyatt was the local hunk and could have his pick from a
harem of willing women. So why was he so interested in Sarah?

Harlequin Presents—the best has just gotten better!
Available in March wherever Harlequin books are sold.

TAUTH-6

Yo amo novelas con corazón!

Starting this March, Harlequin opens up to a whole new world of readers with two new romance lines in SPANISH!

Harlequin Deseo
- passionate, sensual and exciting stories

Harlequin Bianca
- romances that are fun, fresh and very contemporary

With four titles a month, each line will offer the same wonderfully romantic stories that you've come to love—now available in Spanish.

Look for them at selected retail outlets.

HARLEQUIN®

SPANT